HIGH HOLIDAY SUTRA

High Holiday sutra

A NOVEL BY ALLAN APPEL

COFFEE HOUSE PRESS ≋ MINNEAPOLIS

Coffee House Press is supported in part by a grant provided by the Minnesota State Arts Board, through an appropriation by the Minnesota State Legislature, and in part by a grant from the National Endowment for the Arts. Significant support has also been provided by The McKnight Foundation; Lannan Foundation; Jerome Foundation; Target Stores, Dayton's, and Mervyn's by the Dayton Hudson Foundation; General Mills Foundation; St. Paul Companies; Butler Family Foundation; Honeywell Foundation; Star Tribune/Cowles Media Company; James R. Thorpe Foundation; Dain Bosworth Foundation; Pentair, Inc.; Beverly J. and John A. Rollwagen Fund of the Minneapolis Foundation; and many individual donors. To you and our many readers across the country, we send our thanks for your continuing support.

Coffee House Press books are available to the trade through our primary distributor, Consortium Book Sales & Distribution, 1045 Westgate Drive, Saint Paul, MN 55114. For personal orders, catalogs, or other information, write to: Coffee House Press, 27 North Fourth Street, Suite 400, Minneapolis, MN 55401.

LIBRARY OF CONGRESS CIP INFORMATION
Appel, Allan
    High holiday Sutra : a novel / by Allan Appel.
      p. cm.
    ISBN 1-56689-065-9 (pb : alk. paper)
      1. Judaism—Relations—Buddhism—Fiction. 2. Rabbis—United States—Fiction. 3. Jews—United States—Fiction. I. Title.
PS3551.P55H54 1997
813'.54--dc21   97-15992
                                          CIP

10   9   8   7   6   5   4   3   2   1

I am grateful to the following people for their wisdom and help during the writing of this book: my wonderful children Sophia and Nathaniel, Janet Abramowicz, Allen Bergson, Sara Blackburn, my wife Suzanne Boorsch, Marc Kaminsky, Jan Miller, and Peter Minichiello. And to my indispensable teachers, Walter Ackerman, Lloyd Gartner, Rabbi David Lieber, and Eliezer Slomovic, profound thanks and a deep bow.

To the memory of Carolyn Blair Stanek

Judaism's way of repentance is easier than that of other faiths who prescribe bodily self-affliction. Our Torah did not ordain any bodily self-afflictions. Repentance is through the prayer of the lips and the meditations of the heart.

—Isaac Aboab

Do not separate yourself from the community.

—Rabbi Hillel

The long night
The sound of water
Says what I think.

—Gochiku

ALEPH

FRIENDS AND CO-RELIGIONISTS! Devotees of the Hebrew Meditation Circle as well as those of you whose beautiful, puzzled, and sleepy faces I behold for the first time today! Ladies and gentlemen, brothers and sisters! Beloved congregants, welcome!

I call your attention to the Jewish custom on this, the Day of Atonement, Yom Kippur, to read and discuss the brief but gripping Book of Jonah, which you have just heard. For, as you know, Jonah's is a story of forgiveness, flight, cowardice, excruciating self-examination, hypocrisy, the begrudging of God's compassion, depression, and vomiting—

No, no!

Jonah's times, as you have just heard, were the best of times. And they were the worst of times. A time of karma and a time of satori. A time of morality and a time of license.

No, no, no! A flagrant Dickensian rip-off. And will everyone know satori?

Okay. There are many ways to divide up the world: rich and poor, men and women, Hinayana and Mahayana Buddhists, rabbinical and lay, obedient and rebellious, tall and short, regularly-scheduled and chartered, milk and meat, network and cable, gay and straight, forgiving and vengeful, I and Thou, kosher and non, you and me, black and white, Jew and . . .

No, no, no!

Get right to the personal, get to the problem without introduction or mediation.

So. There are great rabbis and pipsqueak rabbis and a whole lot of boring in-between rabbis. I ought to know. I, Rabbi Jonah Grief, am one of them.

That's not the problem. That's the kvetching around the problem!

Okay. Problem: Some of you have already begun to ask, where am I going to take the Hebrew Meditation Circle? What are Rabbi Grief's true values? Why does the word "God" never fall from his lips without agonizing qualification? Just what does it mean when he says he has Jewish feet and Buddhist wings? So many many questions, and I've been with you for what—six weeks?

I've decided that since this is our first Day of Atonement together, today's sermon will bare all: a confession to beat all confessions. When you've heard my command Yom Kippur performance, if I do a good enough job of peeling myself clean for you, layer by layer of my unworthiness, if I am successful in this process of inspiring and touching you with the story of how I came to Zen and zazen, beautiful meditation—and how I planted these flowers in the garden of my Judaism—then perhaps you'll find it within yourselves to accept me at your lovely seaside temple. Oh, I know my past is controversial and perhaps even a little mysterious to some of you, but I vow, on this holy day, to withhold none of it from you. I've only just arrived, we hardly know each other, I feel like a blushing mail-order bride of a rabbi, and the relationship is just beginning, so I hope . . . I hope. Look, I really want to keep this job!

On the other hand, perhaps you will grow exasperated and will decide to dismiss me, send me on. It would not be surprising. Either way, whatever you hear from me, remember that my mind can never fully be on God, on Israel, or even on Buddha's Fourfold Noble Truths and what they have to say about Judaism. Not on Yom Kippur. You see, without your being yet fully aware of it, the confession has already begun.

For, beloved congregants, Yom Kippur, as you know, is the time we not only review and judge our lives but also reflect on mortality and those recently gone. I lost my beloved wife, Ada, shortly before Yom Kippur two years ago. The holy day is therefore forever changed for this rabbi. God tells us not to feel sorry for ourselves in our grieving. Instead we are commanded to praise the Lord and all his creation in the life-affirming Mourner's Kaddish, the Prayer for the Dead, whose verses will endure when this sermon and all sermons are laid to rest.

Personally I much prefer the Zen haiku texts for Yom Kippur, which praise the serene mystery of life and leave God out of it:

If you do not believe,
Look at September!
Look at October.
The yellow leaves falling, falling
To fill both mountains and rivers.

I think particularly on the Day of Atonement that we need flowers and running brooks and wind through the trees. Much more on the Thusness of life, to which God makes not an iota of contribution and even fails as a metaphor.

Yes, I'm starting up with God again and perhaps some of you are already preparing to leave. So soon, Ruthie and Ed? Mel and Tanya? Ah, but, who knows? Blasphemy is in the eye, and ear, of the beholder. As is atonement.

But now, at the midpoint of our afternoon service, please turn with me once again to the Book of Jonah. If you have nothing better to do, stay, listen:

Now the word of the Lord came to Jonah the son of Amittai, saying "Arise, go to Nineveh, that Great City, and cry against it; for wickedness has come up before me." But Jonah rose to flee to Tarshish from the presence of the Lord. He went down to Jaffa and found a ship going to Tarshish; so he paid the fare, and went on board, to go with them to Tarshish, away from the presence of the Lord.

There are many questions we might ask about this passage, far more than we have answers or time for on this Yom Kippur. Why is Tarshish mentioned not one but three times? Why Tarshish at all, as opposed to another city? We might also ask, at the risk of reading modern criminal practices into ancient texts, why Jonah paid his fare, thus leaving a paper trail, as it were, for the Lord to follow. If, however, the Lord, as we say, can read through to each human heart, a little parchment is not going to bother him at all and my question is therefore moot. Moreover, you don't have to be a rabbi to know that illiterate Phoenician sailors are not going to write down *Jonah, Son of Amittai, Twenty-Five Cedar Street.*

Incidentally, where does Jonah come from? What town? Usually when a prophet of the Lord makes his entrance in a biblical text a town is mentioned and sometimes an occupation. For example: "These are the words of Amos, a shepherd from Tekoa." But in the case of Jonah, what do we know about the man? The answer is, precious little. As you know yet precious little about me.

Was Jonah rich or poor? One rabbi says that paying his fare with money proves he was rich or at least middle-class. But who knows? Perhaps he was a thief. And me? Am I going to steal something precious from your wonderful Jewish sangha, your community? Or do I add to it? Questions, questions. The endless commentaries and questions.

And yet Jonah speaks to me through our text, one Jonah to another, and while I certainly don't like

15

him, I can not ignore him. Where, for example, is his argument with the Lord? Where's the tough talking, the kind of bargaining about the fate of the Ninevites that we've come to expect—for example, from Abraham's dealing with God at Sodom and Gomorrah?

What's even Jewish about this Jonah, I ask! Perhaps only his profound sense of persecution and complaint, a kvetcher's mentality. He should have cried, "What the hell do you think you're doing, God?"

Threatening all of Nineveh—one of the greatest cities on earth at the time—and all its people with death, earthquake, destruction! And for what? They don't seem *that* bad. But then here's the rub: You, Lord, changed your mind!

Let me see . . . today we mourn Ben Ziegler, Aphra Smith, Tillie Zimmerman, and may I add Ada Karp Grief, my wife, and all who have passed on. Do not even we, the so-called living, die too, second by self-deluding second? Unless we cock our ears to the drum that is always beating, to the shofar that is always sounding—unless, my congregants, we wake up!

Okay, now let me try a less strident tone for the children's version, for the Junior Congregation sermon; we must have a Junior Congregation. Here goes:

In days gone by, in ancient times long before the Persian Gulf War, children, even before Vietnam and World War ii, back in Bible times, there were heroes. Real heroes. "Who shall go up against the enemy host?" cried the children of Israel as they knocked on the gates of Canaan. And the answer was, Judah shall go up. And did Judah ask for a 4-F, as your rabbi did? Did he get drunk when his lottery number was picked, when his lot was chosen, as Jonah's was later in our story? Did these ancient heroes of ours wear their girlfriends' yellow underwear beneath their tunics, as your rabbi did to his U.S. Army physical that snowy morning in New York City so many bad dreams ago? No, when Judah was called, Judah went up. And Gideon went up, too, another hero, and David, and Deborah, and Ehud, and a whole bunch more, and they smote the Midianites and the Jebusites and the Canaanites . . . and the Stalactites and the Stalagmites. But when Jonah Grief was called, Jonah fled. I, who always wanted only to be a hero, a hero even to myself, I fled.

There are great people, great rabbis, a Mount Rushmore of them, but I know who I am. I am a little weed, far down that mountain, growing in a gravelly patch of grass at the base, scrawny and shifting slightly in the wind. Occasionally I look up.

So stay with me, my assimilated ones, my rushing businessmen and meditating CPAs, you mantra-loving navigators, you wonderful searchers, one and all. And also, please, don't be so itchy. Medieval disputations went on for days. The Puritan preachers harangued their congregations for hours. I look in your eyes and I see that you are edgy. Relax.

My Jewish Buddhists, you are still much too soft. Concentrate as we study together:

> *But the Lord hurled a great wind upon the sea, and there was a mighty tempest on the sea, so that the ship threatened to break up.*

Likewise, Jonah Grief, your spiritual leader. Yet this, my sermon, is the little bark on which you have booked passage with me this Yom Kippur holiday weekend. Think of my sermon as a *sefina,* boat in Hebrew, a cute little word with the connotation of *teensy.* A small vessel, no tanker, perhaps a little Phoenician junk. Such my sermon as well, brave sailors.

Even you, the strong and the healthy ones, maybe have your doubts already. So good-bye, Max, good-bye, Ruby. You look lovely. Is that a new haircut? And mazel tov on the new grandchildren. They make life's circle complete. Isaac, so long! And Francine and Pauline, you remarkable twins, retired ticket agents and part-time palmreaders, possessors of hands that have sent people and the goods of the world millions of miles. I will miss you too. But there are many of you left yet. If you want, I encourage you to leave. Truly. Up, go, do better things. But for you remaining dear friends, hallowed partners in life, chaverim, brothers, sisters, tardy temple-dues-payers, fellow mortals, I'll go on. For what the sermon and the wind-tossed boat of Jonah have in common is that they occasionally lose their way.

But we always find the course again:

Then the mariners were afraid, and each cried to his god; and they threw the wares that were in the ship into the sea, to lighten it for them. But Jonah had gone down into the inner part of the ship and had lain down, and was fast asleep.

Is it not said prophets are dreamers? The beautiful dreamy sleep of childhood, perhaps the farthest place dreams could take Jonah in his flight from the Lord. O Jonah, my namesake and my pal! Please take my hand, as it were, now, and let me bring you back to all my thrilling days of yesteryear, to my growing up not a dozen miles from this very spot. It is about the time *The Lone Ranger* had just come on TV, and your rabbi-to-be lies on the living-room floor, in the bosom and hold of the family ship, riveted, as generations before had been to a page of Talmud, to the electronic page, the newfangled Phillips/Muntz that Victor the Cuban, my father's partner, had provided a full twenty-five dollars below wholesale, twelve-foot-long aerial included at no extra charge.

Your rabbi's youthful elbows are covered with irritating pimples from the purple carpeting, but he will not even become aware of this until the show is over, for he is transfixed by these two heroes, the Masked Man and Tonto—Tonto, who, according to Tommy Slatinsky, son of the Hebrew-school principal, is actually a secret Jew because the

Indians, it is well known, are the Lost Tribes. Even if they're not, Tonto has a lot of Spanish blood in him, which, it is also well established, is commingled with that of the Jews who were expelled from Spain and eventually got to the New World in 1654.

However, when you invert the "6" in 1654, it becomes a "9," as in 1954—in the tradition of geomatria, or numerological exegesis, of our scholarly ancestors—which instantly makes it precisely the year I am describing. I lie comfortably in that year, hearing the rousing *William Tell Overture* punctuate the climactic moments of the story, and Hi-Ho Silver is rearing up and carrying my hero into the sunset, or, at any event, down a dusty winding road toward an optimistic horizon, and a new episode next Thursday night.

Yet I am suddenly in the grip of the profound sadness that comes with the knowledge that as soon as the final credits roll I must telephone twenty kids to persuade them to come to Junior Congregation on the sabbath! I, who only want to be a Lone Ranger, a Masked Man, when I grow up, a bit of a hero. I have to go into the kitchen, find the list from under the bunch of speckled bananas in the breakfast nook, where my father, Mo, short for Maurice, is talmudically poring over the racing form for Santa Anita's daily double tomorrow and might bark at me if I disrupt his concentration. I, who am only the lowly Junior Congregation attendance officer . . . well, the contrast between hope and reality is, as it will be later, nearly too much to bear.

Yet off I go, calling kids at night, interrupting their TV-watching and their family life to remind them how great Junior Congregation is! How we need them for the junior minyan, how the temple needs them and the Hebrew school, the entire community struggling to make a foothold in this Los Angeles seaside diaspora, and God needs them! How could I have said what I said? That an absolutely fascinating section of the Torah is sure to be read. How if you show up a minimum of six times in a row, you also earn a special Junior Cong pin, olive green with a large blue Hebrew letter, to wear on your lapel. Who signed me up for this activity when I should have been playing Little League? Did Sandy Koufax, who was famous among us for refusing to pitch on Yom Kippur, go to Junior Cong? Did he learn his fastball by tossing yarmulkes across the room to kids who came late and without the headgear?

How unbearably square! Yet how early on I must have been recruited—or did I go of my own free will, and, if so, for what reason?—to Junior Cong. So, arise Edith, your rabbi's mother. She comes in and says, "You must call. Here's a pencil, you have the list." How I want to get away and flee like Jonah to the last outpost of land's end, or, if not that, at least through the screen door and down to the corner for an Almond Joy or Snickers at Rappoport's Grocery. "Phone your friends," she says. "Junior Congregation must grow. Rabbi Hall says so every week and he's right. Don't be shy. Check the names off as you go."

Edith is not unattractive in her yellow housecoat that has the slightly fecal scent of jasmine perfume as she sweeps by and supervises my calling Eddie Jellen, the coolest and best-looking kid at school, a pitcher with a real curve at the age of ten, who has the self-confidence and flair of Ed Kookie Burns of *77 Sunset Strip* and future stardom written all over him. Eddie, a guy who, when I go through my line to him about Junior Cong, has to be thinking to himself, this Grief is a complete asshole.

"We look forward to celebrating shabbos with you, Eddie."

"I'm pitching on Saturday, you nitwit," he says. "And you should be playing too, not hustling for the Hebrew school."

Mother knows that if I can get through to Eddie, or merely endure the humiliation of the phone call, then she no longer has to monitor me, that I will carry through and become the Lou Gehrig of Junior Cong. She is therefore up and standing now, beaming a thin stream of pride down upon me, the ink with which an invisible contract is being written. Without my being more than dimly aware of it at the time, my fellow congregants, my deeds were being recorded in the Book of Mothers and Sons and the Book of Families, then to be inscribed later, as you know, through the sale of subsidiary rights, into the Book of Life, both paper and hardcover. My entry says: We both know your father is a ne'er-do-well, a gambler, the black sheep of his family, a kind and decent flop. But this is America, and this is Los

Angeles in the 1950s, and we are in the post-war boom; upward mobility is sweeping everybody along—everybody except your Damon Runyonesque dad, whose brothers are all doctors active in their synagogues while he does God knows what with Victor and those Cubans in the produce market by day and gambles by night at the poker tables. His idea of Jewish affiliation is corned beef on rye.

Additional text: "After what happened in Europe," she says to me as I continue to make my calls and she clearly detects a new and threatening reluctance, "it's important for every Jewish boy to go to Hebrew school, especially in this spiritual wasteland." Echoing Rabbi Hall of the synagogue, whom she admires beyond all measure, she says, "We live in a place full of people out to convert us, full of Mormons and Father Divines and Jehovah's Witnesses and Paramahansa Yoganandas. Promise me you will never pray with them, Jonah."

"I promise."

"Promise me you will marry only a Jewish girl."

"I promise, I promise."

"I'll speak to Eddie's mother myself. She'll understand, woman to woman."

"No, please, Mom. Let it go. I'll talk to him in school," I beg.

"All right. You'll have more success with the others."

And of course I did.

To prove it, I have, as some of you have already seen, who have had the thrill of visiting me here in my study—by the way, you're all invited, no appointment necessary—my green, yellow, and blue Junior Cong pins proudly displayed, plus the aleph and gimmel, the hey, chet, and tet pins as well. Six years of Junior Cong. Six years of calling and Edith beaming down upon me such approval that when I've hung up after each success, she comes in and tells me how charming I am, what talent I have in speaking to people, what effortless ease, how great and important such work is for our little L.A. diaspora. Where did I learn such smooth and endearing ways? And, ladies and gentlemen, so much praise settles down over my profound unease and embarrassment that it mixes like odd chemicals into a strange gas of responsibility, pride, and ambition; and in that gas, somewhere, beloved congregants, your rabbi-to-be was born.

It would be many years before Junior Cong was replaced in your rabbi's consciousness by Viet Cong, when the Vietnam War lottery was under way. How did he do then, your rabbi, when he was in college and trying for the first time truly to practice what our prophets preached?

Alas, don't you already know, my sleepy ones? We stood on the steps at Columbia University, to which the L.A. Jewish community's scholarship had sent me, and we shrieked and grabbed garbage cans and dropped them on police cars and barricaded buildings and soaped steps so that the Tactical Patrol Force might break their hips in trying to apprehend us. It was not that we loved the Viet Cong but that those of us in Students for a Democratic Society had forgotten the values of Junior Cong, and we got no guidance from our rabbis, or our professors, who were as confused as we but also hampered in their will and political resolve by knowing far more history. But these episodes will occur many years later.

Have we any takers this afternoon for the hypothesis that the Jonah of our text was himself a very young man, perhaps even a teenager? Per-haps a bar mitzvah boy on the run? With what heart-pounding anxiety your rabbi turned thirteen. Yes, congregants should be curious about their rabbi's evolving spirituality, for is not spirituality based, initially, on a generalized and emerging unease, an anxiety that, before it finds its way later in life to the discovery of the mysterium tremendum, is in short profoundly grounded in the very concrete fear of how one will do at his bar mitzvah? Are we not curious about our doctors' illnesses and our dentists' cavities? Would you continue to see a dentist whose breath stinks, whose molars are rotting, and whose very own gums show traces of strain and blood even while he's working over you? You are therefore legitimately curious about your rabbi's bar mitzvah and other rites of passage, and I will not disappoint you.

O, beloved daughters and sons of the holy covenant of Abraham, Isaac, and Jacob, etc., I will not make it easy for you to dismiss me by offering up stock jokes about my bar mitzvah. For one week before the long-anticipated event I was up on Hollywood Boulevard with Mo, where he usually met his bookie. As I stood there I saw the eye of God, a giant hazel pupil the size of the moon, peeping through a cumulus swirl just above the "o" in the HOLLYWOOD sign. I took my father's hand, which I had not done in years, and I squeezed tight. Oh, I feared the Lord at age thirteen, as Jonah did, precisely because He was in the heavens, on the dry land, everywhere, even in Hollywood. It could not be clearer that if I did something wrong, sooner or later I would be caught. Therefore, why flee?

I wanted—I needed—to have a perfect bar mitzvah. Although I could not carry a tune then or now (is this why the low, grounded, tuneless Buddhist chants fit in my voice box like a hand in a glove?), still I knew my portion cold, every Hebrew word, including derivations. I had even aced a few commentaries on my portion. I intended to be flawless for the Lord. For, as many of you know, if you read a line from the Torah and mispronounce even a word or skip one, you must go back and correct your error. Each and every word must be read accurately. If it's not, what's the consequence? Then the Lord knows that something else was on your mind, maybe the Dodgers game, or your girlfriend, your job, your constipation—it matters not, because if the word is wrong and uncorrected and He is impatient, like Rabbi Hall and like my father, it could lead, who knew, to the end of the world! At least I did not croak the melodies like the old men, like Mr. Ginsberg with his rasping, potatoey voice. And because I did get everything right, I knew God would not mind that the only way I could get through the singing was to fake the nigun, the melody, making believe I was sort of the Chuck Berry of Torah reading.

So I pleased the Lord. I knew it, and yet by earthly standards the ceremony was a flop. Why? Not because of my tunelessness or the usual reasons a contemporary bar mitzvah fails—the parents' tastelessness in leasing the Queen Mary for a floating bar mitzvah soirée or retaining an Elvis look-alike to do a rock-and-roll Hava Nagila. Oh no! The central memory of this rabbi's bar mitzvah has been and will always remain the damage caused to the ceremony's glory by my cousin Rachel's nipples.

There she is: She floats up on the waves of memory in her chair to the right of the Holy Ark, she the bat mitzvah, wrapped in enough pink chiffon, petticoats, and swaths of muslin that she crinkles with each step. "Rachel, bas Avraham v'Sarah," sings out Rabbi Hall, while I am sitting to the left of the Holy Ark sweating bullets in my brown bar mitzvah suit. I wonder in my thirteen-year-old fashion how I will ever be able to follow beautiful Rachel's act and bless my blessings and read my readings, because the Cong will still be remembering Rachel, who precedes me.

Most impossible for me to compete with are Rachel's pubescent breasts, the sharp tips of her nipples, as I remember them even now, growing more dramatic by the minute, with every cantillation, with each sibilant Hebrew sound she intones in her beautiful soprano. Growing and pushing through the bodice of her dress, visible above the lectern, where she is surrounded by rabbis, cantors, and old men suddenly feeling young and coltish, Rachel's nipples seem to be everywhere.

Nevertheless, when it was my turn, I somehow rose and commenced to read my portion. I followed the silver-fingered pointer that Mr. Ginsberg held in his palsied grip. I had prepared so thoroughly that the actual reading was a letdown. But on I went, chanting my way into our three-thousand-year-old tradition, mimicking the moves of my elders in prayer just as Eddie Jellen mimicked Junior Gilliam's quick and graceful steps at shortstop, and hoping against hope that I would not be rejected either because of my croaking or, by way of overcompensation, because of the awful straining in my voice.

All the while I read, however, Rachel's presence surrounded me as the waters surrounded Jonah. She had sat down beside the ark emptied of the Torah and was leaning toward us at the lectern.

What is the allure of Torah reading, I ask you, compared to a thirteen-year-old girl bursting into puberty and leaning your way? My cousin can barely conjugate basic Hebrew verbs! She has never shown up at Junior Cong, whereas I have *lived* there. And this morning, when I ascend from Junior to Senior Cong wearing all my pins on my lapel under my prayer shawl and look to finally achieve full public recognition as the hope of Israel and the diaspora of Los Angeles, I realize that no one is paying the slightest attention to me!

Who has agreed to this arrangement? Where is the rabbi-to-be's father, who is splitting expenses with his brother, Rachel's dad, on the reception to be held at Smokey Joe's Taproom and saving many bucks for the track at great emotional cost to his son? To him I should have cried, with all the indignation of foreknowledge, as the mariners had cried to Jonah:

What is this that you have done?

My father the culprit did not even walk with us to shul on that bar mitzvah morning! He was out at Santa Anita playing the horses far later than usual on Friday night and badly overslept, so that no amount of my mother's prodding could wake him. Just as I was about to be called up to the dais by Rabbi Hall, Mo arrived, panting, at the sanctuary door. He tried to catch his breath—the whole congregation thought he was dying—when I, up there all alone on stage, *I* was dying! When he recovered, he waved to us and then to the congregation, as if it were *his* audience, and then theatrically touched his hirsute hand to the boxy mezuzah on the sanctuary jamb and kissed it.

Anyway, beloveds, my mother shot him a terrible look. Rachel's father—his older brother who knows him all too well—acknowledged with an exasperated exchange that at least the black sheep has had the basic decency to show up, and I, who have been raised to compensate for my father's wayward style, wished that instead of showing up at my own coming of age, he were anywhere but here.

So wait, dear friends, fellow congregants, descendants of Judah and Jesse, there is more! Dear temple-goers and friends, dear members of sisterhood and brotherhood committees, my beloved colleagues in the fellowship of Zen, Theravadas and Tibetans and devotees of the tea ceremony and the Noh plays, dear women's auxiliary presidents, and chevra kadishas and bikur cholim societies, past, present, and future. Dear Jewish groups of all kinds and all times, when I with my croaking adolescent voice finally quieted, and with Rachel sexy and triumphant behind me, as I stood above our holy Torah, the sea of knowledge, the line upon line of black waves of text, when now the moment had arrived for my haftorah and, following it, my formal speech thanking teachers and parents and praising the joys of community, what I instead began to consider was having a public nervous breakdown. I had read about breakdowns in Edith's *Life* magazine and *Reader's Digest,* and it seemed to me to be so close to my daily experience that having one on the dais, combined with my bar mitzvah, might not only be novel but appropriate. Surely if

Rachel could turn her bat mitzvah effectively into a Miss Teenage America pageant, why couldn't I suddenly become a Jewish Jimmy Dean: smash the ark, hurl a prayer book and knock out the eternal light, laugh at old Mr. Ginsberg, and then advance on Rabbi Hall with a sharp and broken Torah pointer as he is suddenly transfigured into Karl Malden?

I am still considering, even after all these years: to dive in or not to dive in, that is the question. Oh, I knew Eddie Jellen, who had the hots for Rachel, was somewhere out in the back rows of the sanctuary waving his baseball glove at me every now and then during my speech when the ushers were not looking, as if in some petty sacrilegious way God through Eddie seemed to be saying to me: Jonah Grief, bar mitzvah boy, harken unto me! This day I offer you Torah or baseball. Choose, you!

Fact is, dear Eddie and my indulgent congregants, God, who appreciates the nearly perpetual puerility of His creatures, does not call us the Children of Israel for nothing. For every word, for every phrase a reason. Not the Adults but the Children, the Babies of Israel. My dream, I said, in my bar mitzvah remarks, was to become a great baseball player and Jewish scholar. And, I asserted, there was no contradiction. This was my first sermon, my bar mitzvah speech that day.

I went on: Baseball was, after all, a profession where you wore your hat, and a proudly religious Jewish ballplayer would fit in nicely, straight-faced, earnest, and truthful. Such a figure would balance out the many superstitious and demonstrably Christian players who crossed themselves just before kicking dirt and stepping into the batter's box. As such, I preached that no prohibition against playing on the sabbath would stand the test of religious law as scrutinized and interpreted by my venerable pre-rabbinic self. I would quote like mad from sources across a thousand years of scholarship. I would demonstrate to the best legal halachic minds that for Jonah Grief, the pious new infield sensation of the L.A. Dodgers, since the game was not work but pure pleasure, playing was not only permissible on the sabbath but encouraged.

In fact I would have my best games on the day of rest, on those Saturday afternoons, after Junior Cong, when the world seemed quite nearly perfect and full of exquisite promise. Oh yes, I will step into that world again now. I will stride up to the plate, perhaps, in my rookie season. My tsis tsis, the tassels of my little prayer shawl, will dangle out from under my Dodger blue uniform, and just as Warren Spahn leans in for his sign I will twirl them to distract him. As the pitch comes spinning toward me, I will intone the sacred sounds of the Shemah Yisroel. Just as I utter the last Hebrew word, on the wings of those holy vowels, I will stroke a classic single into center. Then I steal second and come home on Wally Moon's liner hit just beyond Joe Adcock's outstretched glove at first.

After our victory, and basking in the growing respect of my teammates, I pray mincha, the afternoon service, in a corner of the sweaty locker room. Before the season is out, with my average hovering around .400, my fielding record equalling that of Honus Wagner, my steals those of Ty Cobb, and a hitting streak of 51 games threatening Joe Dimaggio's, the team, en masse, led by the Silver Fox, Duke Snyder, will suddenly become keenly interested in Judaism. Former anti-Semitic attitudes melt away. Then, my congregants, on the day we whip the Yankees four straight to win the World Series, in a solemn ceremony at home plate of the just-completed Dodger Stadium—whose infield green that day will look like the front yard of heaven—every single member of the team will convert to Judaism.

Ladies and gentlemen, my dear friends, Rachel, Rachel, I chose not the glove but our Torah. Do you remember my speech, Rachel? I do yours. Is your bat mitzvah as vivid to you as it is to me? Do you think of it as often as I do, as you write advertising copy and volunteer at the hospital? Or do you teach literature and decorate your house and care for your children and your husband—we've been out of touch so long! Isn't he that nice neurologist who treated Mr. Ginsberg and saintly Dr. Lubliner too before they died?

Ah, those teachers of mine. They, beyond all other influences, made me adore Hebrew school and landed me in this spot where I am this very day! And let us not slight Rabbi Hall, who had a massive coronary during kiddush on Succot ten years ago, collapsed onto a table full of sponge and honey cake, and it has been said since that he provided the model, even in death, for the way to go: fast and soft.

Are you out there before me this day, this Yom Kippur, my adored ones, my teachers, my roshis, yoga experts, friends, worshippers, fellow K-Mart shoppers, and compromisers in life? Are you there, Jews? Meditators? People of the Book, all of you, wake up!

For they said to Jonah, chapter 1, verse eleven:

What shall we do to you that the sea may quiet down for us?

And he answered them, "Muzzle me! Or I will tell you about the rest of my absurd and misspent life in the service of the Lord, which is what has pissed His Mightiness off to begin with, and it surely will drive you mariners to the breaking point as well." Yes, indeed. Do not think for a moment that because Jonah's full response went unrecorded in his Book that it did not occur. To my eye, the Book of Jonah reads like one of the most censored, worked-over texts of antiquity. We do have a tradition of confession, only it was cut short.

So I am here on this Yom Kippur weekend filling in all blanks, dissecting myself for you in honor of the cut Jonah. You know the practice, my meditators: We begin at the skin, then go into it, via meditation, down to the bone. From the bone we descend to the organs. Here you see my heart, open before you again, looking like a piece of red granite schist.

"The sea will quiet down for you," Jonah said. For *you,* but certainly not for *me.* And why should it! Thus we are always at sea, and it is now in my story, my congregants, the year 1966. The years of the Vietnam War lottery are at hand. Your rabbi-to-be is in a dark bar on 114th Street in New York City, eight blocks from the Seminary, nearly broke, lonesome, and afraid. He has on his green Eisenhower jacket, smelling pleasantly of camphor, taken from Mo's closet, and a baseball cap over his yarmulke—a secularizing habit you will no doubt recognize—when someone, drunk, begins railing about Vietnam and how he had seen with his own eyes the way G.I.s make severed Viet Cong ears into pouches. The war would end fast if people saw *that* on TV, he pronounced.

Your rabbi-to-be, then a college student, Seminary bound, your future ringmaster of justice and ethics, only nodded in neutral agreement. More beer was ordered, and the jukebox played Country Joe and the Fish, and a police car raced by outside, the arc of its alarm rising and receding.

Then a small man in a green jacket, who up to now had said little, quietly spoke up. "They do it to us," was all he said, turning so we saw that he was not in an army surplus uniform like ours, but was real army, and he had several medals above his pocket that picked up the faint bar light. When he took a sip of beer, we noticed that the sleeve of his neatly pressed jacket was pinned up to his shoulder. With his right hand he raised his mug of beer. "To peace," he said quietly to us. "To peace."

I finished my beer and drank another and another. "To peace," was all he said, and yet those words were an eloquent sermon in themselves, the best I've ever heard preached. A sermon most suited to 1966, which was a time when the idealism on which we had grown up and soared began to lose altitude fast—8,000 feet, 7,000 feet, we're not going to make it, sir! Out of gas, out of luck . . . until POW! CRASH! like a Sergeant Rock comic, the idealism hits the ground, torn apart, destroyed. And now we pick through it—that's what a sermon is for, no?—trying to identify idealism's remains, hoping there are at least some vital parts left.

You see what I've done! A typical homiletical trick. I start a personal story just to capture or retain your flagging attention. Then I obliterate my particularity completely in the universalism called for by the sneaky sermon genre. I generalized, I felt this impulse to connect with the year, the zeitgeist. It's not enough that I was a fool in the bar disguising my rabbinical identity beneath a baseball hat. Not enough to nod in what could be interpreted as agreement with the racist and imperialist opinions of a drunk. What I felt when the soldier turned to us—handsome, dark-eyed, proud—was simply that I wanted to be him. I wanted, God help me, to exchange my life for his. How can a soul in which such an impulse resides survive in rabbinical school?

There had to be a way I could help. We were very drunk by then, this soldier and your rabbi-to-be, who insisted on buying him all his drinks with what remained of my scholarship. Then he said to me, "There's plenty of civilians ferrying cargo down the Mekong. You don't have to be in uniform to get shot at. Why do you want to get shot at anyway?" he asked.

I thought for a long time and said, "It just seems right."

By the time we stumbled outside, it was three A.M., and Broadway was fairly empty. As we stood there beside the bus post, I wanted to put my arm over his shoulder. It would have given the episode closure and meaning—and above all I needed meaning! I imagined myself doing it but I didn't dare. For I had two arms and he had only one, and the bus lumbered up then. So we shook hands awkwardly and said goodnight, and he might have lived and he might have died.

Down to this very day, I still keep alive that moment and my adolescent dream of sailing down the Mekong to be shot at. To survive, of course, to have some slight blood loss and perhaps even a scar. And lately my daydream takes this form: While I am up here making my milk-toast sabbath remarks, a bright congregant, perhaps one of you, will simply snap. Perhaps it will be my soldier himself. Quite by chance he is in town on business and will have seen, in crooked letters on the marquee outside, my name and the starting time of the services. He listens to my ecclesiastical kvetching and particularly the way I have shaped this incident of his life differently from his recollection, the way I have squeezed the truth into a kind of sabbath and holy-day broth that I ladle out to you to flatter your sense of worldliness and history.

As he listens he becomes outraged at the distortions he is hearing. Suddenly he withdraws the weapon he carries in his pocket, raises it safely above your yarmulked heads, and finally puts this sermon, along with its perpetrator, out of its misery. As I collapse, I hear our cantorial student, Randy Margolies, screaming for someone to call 911, but I have just enough strength to run forward and throw my arms around my good soldier, at last. At that moment a small kind of satori, an awakening, occurs, and your rabbi's world expands exponentially. How I wish!

Please be with me next week for other exciting biographical episodes full of Zen-like wonder: why your rabbi-the-boy was convinced nuns spoke Yiddish but astronauts could not, and how my friend Martin was so overcome with an impulse to sacrilege, not unlike your rabbi-to-be, that he exposed himself in the synagogue one summer day at Camp Tikvah and was tossed out. Please be with me for many a thrilling incident from those days and these more recent days too. For it *is* as you are thinking; I confess: the rabbi wanders all over his life, as the Jews wandered in the desert, looking for signs and miracles of their God and for their promised land. For he has the chutzpah to turn his life into his own puny little ill-written, mistake-riddled Torah and to leaf through it, a sentence here, a chapter, an incident there, elucidating the hidden meanings, the numerologies, the derivations. And all on the specious premise that ontogeny recapitulates phylogeny. Now what was the name of that soldier? Was it Bruce Roberts? Was it Roger? Was it Able? Baker? Charlie? Dog? In the meantime may God bless you and keep you. May He cause his countenance to shine down upon you and give you peace.

Perhaps the fact that so far we have not seen that much of each other keeps our relationship fresh. If I were your regular longtime rabbi, if I had circumcised your baby boys, bar and bat mitzvahed your sons and daughters, married and buried you, then you would perhaps hold me to a higher standard. So far your lack of supervision, your distance from me, your apparent satisfaction, thus far, with our sabbath and meditation services that occasionally make the local paper, might be very risky, even dangerous. Some of you, I know, have heard what happened at the United Hebrew Alliance of Kleinkill, my last position. You chuckle. Nevertheless, are we not creating, in the opinion of some independent observers yet to be identified, a twelve-headed rabbinical Shiva that must be stopped before anti-Semitism has new targets, before it is too late for the community, Israel, and the planet? You chuckle once again. Yes, I admire your adventurous spirit, my friends, and I hope that together we can sustain it. Please!

Come back to me now, my own wonderful teachers—Lubliner, Wiesner, and Becker, you who are veterans of World War II, or its refugees. When you finally came to L.A., all you wanted was to stay still, to read most of the day and night, to have your wives back and wear dry socks, to *not* be shot at ever again or be chased by Nazis or by any force more threatening than disobedient and disrespectful Hebrew-school students. It was no wonder you were such excellent teachers, you who were inspired by a mission to build a Jewish community here on these shifting Pacific sands. A brief bill of particulars:

—Walter Becker, why did I learn three, maybe four times from you about the Minor Prophets? About Amos the shepherd from Tekoa, Amos the patron saint of earthquakes and of Jewish life along the San Andreas Fault. I ask you, is this to be desired? He preached in the reign of King Uzziah, two years before the Great Noise. Was it because the Great Noise, the earthquake, struck several times during your class, knocking our books from the shelves? And because of it, I was able to help up Tina Levine, our beautiful hora dancer and in the process notice her perfect thigh? Was this the reason? If so, my eternal gratitude.

—Ray Wiesner, you are responsible for the Timed Speed Reading of the Shemah Yisroel. You took the holiest Jewish prayer, the declaration of faith—Shemah Yisroel Adonai Elohenu Adonai Echad, Hear O Israel, the Lord Our God, the Lord is One—along with the blessing and the paragraph of instructions that followed in the siddur and had us read as fast as nine-year-old tongues and lips could move. One second added for each garbled or skipped word. I, class star as usual, broke the ribbon at the Shemah finish line in 33 seconds! Let the sound track from *Chariots of Fire* roll! What, I ask you, was the reason for this exercise, this Shemah Olympics? The impatience that comes from freeway living? Wiesner, what was the rush?

—Michael Lubliner, angelic skin and sparkling eyes from another world of kindness, tufts of nose hair and whiskers as you smiled down over us like a big Hasidic Cheshire cat. Your sins are two: First, you were a mad tree planter for Israel and made me risk my gambler father's ire when I filled eighteen pushkas full of coins for you, setting a record I believe is still unbroken in the Los Angeles Hebrew-school system. There must be some records I still hold! Second sin, and more severe, Michael: because I was first to master the Hebrew vowels you taught, you set me up at your desk every afternoon to help the other kids while you went out of the room. This anointing of me as a Young Vowel Expert has no doubt profoundly affected not only my relation with other men, who perhaps are not as up on the vowels as I am, but also the career choice I suffer from now. Why did you have to leave the room? Were you praying? A bladder condition? Calling your broker on a poor cheyder teacher's modest salary?

However, this conundrum first: If a boring rabbi reads these words in an empty congregation, walking from the dais to his study nearby, some eight feet from the Holy Ark, reading aloud, pausing for an answer from the empty hall, getting none, but continuing—was there then a sermon? If the Holy One, Blessed be He or She, appears to the crummiest rabbi in the land, the most unaccomplished scholar, and if the person to whom revelation has occurred has himself never believed in the concept and could not ever accept it and still can not—even though he knows something unique is happening to him—how can anything tangible or authoritative be said to have happened?

If, in short, our faith, history, and persecution breed profound skepticism, defensiveness, a show-me attitude, where the search is far more important in itself than anything that might actually be found, then, dear brothers and sisters, Kids of the Kovenant, then how can we have faith left, we, a nation of fakers? Stiff-necked ones that no amount of health-clubbing will cure. We who yearn for faith but can only find comedy. We who pooh-pooh the mumbo jumbo but still yearn for spirituality. We who would like to understand heaven but, when we conceive of it, see only a kind of full-service retirement home, a vast cerulean Miami or Phoenix. If I do not mix milk with meat, will I then feel the sacredness of life? We are lost in details. When you ask me about heaven and hell or why bad things happen to good people, and I tell you to find the Buddha within you and read a little Rabbi Akiba while you're at it, is that what you ultimately want? I certainly want more. I want. I crave. I desire, and I suffer! Yes, it is tough to be a Jew. In our faith we demand that everyone carry out 613 commandments. We demand that everyone therefore strive to be a kind of priest. That is an impossible ideal, even for the tough among us. And I am not tough enough. I am a Laurel and Hardy of rabbis, no great loss at all, a Charlie Chaplin of chaplains. This is why I need to have you hear the story of my past, to have you truly know your Jonah. Briefly, I promise.

Why am I so good at asking questions, so poor at answering? Where is the fruit of Sonoma, my children? Where is the pride of Sacramento, the Manischevitz, the plum brandy, the slivovitz of inspiration?

Draw not the wrong conclusion, Max and Randy, Edith and Pete, Joanne and Dahlia, Abe and Sara, blessed Dr. Lubliner and Rabbi Wiesner, and sainted Rambam, Steve Bilko, Wally Moon, Moe Berg, Walter Becker, Ruthie Galazter, my eleven-year-old love from Camp Tikvah, Mordecai Emanuel Noah, about whom I cribbed several term papers, Felix Frankfurter, Tommy, Eddie, Uncle Si, Aunt Estelle, Saadia Gaon, Shimon Peres, Edith and Mo, mother and father, my teachers, Rachel,

Brandy Lee, most of all my Ada, my beloved departed wife. Friendly congregational ears, past, present, future, yo! Dudes! Ta ushema! Listen up! Because I'd love to stay here if you'll let me.

BET

So they took up Jonah and threw him into the sea; and the sea ceased from its raging. Then the men feared the Lord exceedingly, and they offered sacrifice to the Lord and made vows.

And the Lord appointed a great fish to swallow up Jonah; and Jonah was in the belly of the fish three days and three nights.

Great fish of marriage, you are Brandy Lee—nicknamed Wild Thing—Snyder, the rabbi's first wife. You are evolutionary spirit-relative of Jonah's fish as surely as his life and soul repeat themselves in me and fill me with his wild, driven Jewish karma.

It is no wonder I vowed vows with you.

Yet notice how reticent of details is our original text. We don't know what kind of fish she was, no hint of the species that saved Jonah. Was she expecting a great challenge to her abilities and then when she, at God's beck and call, finally arrived alongside this bobbing, nearly lifeless human morsel of a Jonah, smaller and less appetizing than a squid, did she think to herself, for this I have traveled three oceans? Did the creature have no emotions? Although this is the major physical and dramatic action of the story, do we not finish it knowing little? Do we not know far more about Monstro and Pinocchio than we do about the great fish of my namesake? Alas, the narrative here is characteristic of biblical style: extreme abbreviation of detail, and dramatic reticence to an irritating degree. Yet one thing is clear in my mind, and that is that she, the great fish, is female—maternal, amniotic, all-embracing, watery woman.

Sensing also that we get far less than we need from God, the original author of the ichthyological drama, the rabbis have written that the great fish didn't just *happen* to be swimming the warm Mediterranean and get recruited by the Lord to keep our hero from drowning. According to commentators whose names I have forgotten, God had fashioned the great fish way back during the six days of creation precisely for this purpose. Indeed, she had been waiting around all this time, without being allowed to make friends or to mate, just so she would be in prime condition to rescue Jonah. Can you believe, all those years, all those geological eras of waiting and swimming and growing bored! Therefore her great pent-up powers, her not-to-be-denied planfulness, and her smooth faultless execution of her rescue mission. So, thus inspired by our rabbis, it is not difficult for me to fill in other details.

Brandy Lee, my great green fish, was a daughter in a fourth-generation American Jewish family that had helped to settle the Midwest. The Snyders were also distinguished for having achieved entrepreneurial success without assimilation. If there was any problem for Brandy, apart from the heavy burden of greatness and expectation, it was that she was a daughter in a family of sons. The sons became known for their various religious "firsts": the first documented Jewish family to produce a child in Ohio, the first to light the sabbath candles west of the Mississippi, the first Jewish family to conduct a ritual circumcision and persist in completing the ceremony beneath a Conestoga wagon in spite of an Indian raid that threatened to rain arrows down on them. A family that for generations had expected greatness from their children, and the progeny always delivered.

In many ways, Brandy Lee was the greatest of them. The problem was that my Brandy, the real Brandy, born in 1947, was a woman from an era not yet ready to accept all of her. Nevertheless, she left her home in Pawnee Junction, Kansas, at age eighteen, in 1965, and enrolled at Barnard College. From Barnard, she was only six short blocks away from the Jewish Theological Seminary, where she enrolled for additional courses in Hebrew and Talmud. Here she was in close proximity to the next great generation of the lights of the diaspora. One of these would become her husband. As it turned out to be yours truly, I will be the first to agree what a loss it was to the Snyders. Nevertheless, it must also be said that at the time of which we speak, Brandy Lee felt herself possessed of such powers to love, to teach, to uplift, to correct, to kiss and embrace, and to cure that only someone in my dire straits could have been worthy of her awesome scholarly, resuscitative, and seductive talents. With anyone more pulled together, Brandy simply could not have felt fully herself.

Here is what Brandy was wearing when I first set eyes on her in 1968, during registration at the Seminary: tight Levis of normal length—although summer would transform them into butt-hugging cutoffs—and a clinging sweater of pastel-colored Angora, knitted by one of the pioneer bobbes, hanging loosely above a cowboy belt so that when Brandy bent or stooped, her healthy skin, the color of eighteen-dollar-per-pound whitefish, was delectably visible. The centerpiece of this fine belly was a deep button, an omphalos, perhaps an inch above the belt, that was an erotic wonder in its own right, because for Brandy foreplay always began at this central location. More on this later. I insert the point here only to jog certain of my weaker-souled, but no less loved, congregants whose sermon-listening, book-reading, TV-viewing, child-rearing, cooking, and leisure-time activities, alas, require a regular peppering of titillation to maintain attention.

To continue, she wore hand-tooled cowboy boots. I believe they were alligator skin. Atop all this and giving it a chaotic kind of coherence was Brandy's wild mountain of red hair held up in back by an immense turquoise comb imported from Israel, of course, so that the hair fell out from its great never-ending reservoir and meandered down half her body length, pooling at the small of her back like a red inland sea.

In a holy if dusty precinct such as the Seminary, in those times of which I speak, when the women we students saw most were so much like our revered mothers—shy, middle-aged secretaries working a first job, kindly and energetic folk-dance teachers, exhausted rabbis' wives; with pleasant, rouged faces, and expressions of lively protectiveness toward us; with roughened yet Jergens-Lotioned and capable hands that have koshered and fried many a chicken; with bodies thickly swathed in pimply white stockings, loosely hanging black and brown skirts, and roomy peasant blouses—in short, where female sartorial modesty was not only a style but a mitz-vah, a commandment, Brandy Lee's arrival for registration that fall day struck us like the setting down of a Kansas cyclone.

With her healthy, slightly hoydenish, and ringing laugh she caused major rabbinical traffic jams and relieved those long, torpid afternoon hours waiting in the A-to-L or the M-to-Z lines in the Seminary's waxed corridors. Rabbinical students in advanced stages of their pursuit of the mysterium tremendum startled and woke up, as if the revelation at Sinai had suddenly occurred again, rending solitary historical time and shocking them into acute and new physical sensations. They fell over themselves to be helpful to Brandy, to introduce themselves, to draw her a map of the campus, to peruse the catalogue, or to provide the intimate lowdown on a famous philosopher who though a brilliant writer was a mediocre instructor—to do just about anything for the thrill of standing near her.

Although I was clearly one of Brandy's many admirers, I, for some reason that I did not discover until the harrowing early days of our marriage, preferred to admire her from some distance. Don José to her Carmen, in the beginning I just stared, respectful and even a little fearful, as I would behold any considerable force of nature.

Yes, dear graduates of the University of 1960s, College of Top Forty Tunes, I know it seems a cliché, but it is a truer-than-true one. On that peculiarly sex-starved theological corner, at 122nd Street and Broadway (Cantor Margolies, please begin to hum loudly the Drifters' tune "On Broadway"), Brandy wasn't only Brandy; for a while she was indeed w-o-m-a-n. For she was every 1960s rabbi's fantasy: a cheerleader and prom queen you could not only study Torah with, but really learn from! A true centerfold with more between the ears than Rabbis Hillel and Shammai!

As it turned out, she and I both enrolled in Rabbi Greenwald's Intermediate Talmud. After three weeks of effortlessly showing us how much she knew, she turned down Rabbi Greenwald's suggestion that

she switch to a more advanced class, and was desig-
nated Answer Woman by Greenwald, much as I had
been anointed Vowel Boy by Michael Lubliner. She
was obviously very uncomfortable, but Greenwald
pressured her to remain in this role, in part, of course,
to humiliate us.

So we began to avoid both Greenwald's and
Brandy's eyes. Most of us—including my closest
friends and fellow Talmud sufferers, Big Lou
Hartman, Arthur, and Ronnie, whom I will soon
tell you about—preferred to endure our own puzzlement in embarrassed silence or ratchet up our
ignorance to some point of self-induced knowledge
or illumination, where we might at least begin to
offer a fumbling answer to Rabbi Greenwald's
inquiries. As lessons progressed, or rather continued, because progress was nowhere in sight for
many of us, the atmosphere grew so tense I felt I
was awaiting a sudden bombardment; it was only a
matter of when the missiles would hit.
Occasionally Brandy tried to lessen our torment
with her sympathetic glance.

My fellow congregants and lifelong learners, I am
not talking about an impossibly difficult or arcane
text that lay before us in Intermediate Talmud One;
it was tractate Baba Metzia, which Brandy, incidentally, had mastered at age thirteen with the help of
her father, the president of Kansas Tool & Dye, and
one of the major Talmudists of the Midwest. You
remember Baba Metzia, do you not, my Jewish and
Buddhist brothers and sisters, meditators, beloved

Hebrew-school dropouts one and all? A man approaches a corner carrying an amphora of wine on his head. Another approaches from the side street, this one with a long plank of wood balanced over his shoulder. It is a blind corner. Bam! The plank hits the jug, which falls and cracks; bye bye, wine. Who, now, is responsible? Max Plank? Of course, Max should have shouted ahead that the wood was coming. But should not Jughead also have anticipated a possible collision and taken precautions when approaching a blind corner? What level of compensation is called for? And do we let it go at property damage? What about compensation for being made a fool of? Damages are calculated in seven different categories, at varying levels, and all of this in third-century Hebrew and Aramaic, mixed with a little Latin and Greek, while Rabbi Greenwald patrols the aisles like a farmer seeding the rows with unanswerably difficult questions.

"What do you think, Miss Snyder?" he finally cried in frustration. "The future rabbis of America have joined together in a union of ignorance! They have time to help the renegades and young communists at Columbia in a rent strike but no time left to master a simple page of Talmud! Students for a Democratic Society indeed," he sneered. Dr. Greenwald was unabashedly conservative and fearful of the student revolution brewing six blocks to the south. "Is it of no significance that those of you who know the least about Gemarah seem to know the most about breaking the law? Grief, would you rather break a law, or study it?" Before he had even a chance to take in my helpless shrug, he turned his back on me, and then appealed to Brandy, using her Hebrew name, which means Wild Living Thing, "Chaya, please help these boys out of the pit of their ignorance."

Brandy answered forthrightly, with clarity, succinctness, and a logic that, as always, never concealed her brilliance or good cheer; yet she was no Madame Defarge exulting in our fate. Greenwald, able to add little or nothing to her faultless excursus, always gave Brandy a respectful little bow from the waist, like a European butler.

It won't surprise you to hear that fate had provided for me to be directly in Greenwald's firing line the day he hurled a book—a paperback—at us in one of his exhibitions of contempt. "You caught the bouquet," Brandy Lee said to me out in the hall. "That usually means you'll marry soon."

"The only marrying I'm doing," I managed to utter with some feeble liturgical wit, "is tomorrow, when the sabbath Bride arrives as always."

"So nice to hear," Brandy said, "that She is your steady date. Are you sure there is no other?"

I averted my eyes from her dark, breathing belly button, the Zen rise and fall of all life, at her abdomen's center, the in-breath and out-breath of all creation. I shook my head. "None other."

"You know, don't you, that the Sabbath Bride is the Shechinah personified, the female aspect of God in Kabala? If the dating gets serious, you'll be making love with God—symbolically, of course."

I swallowed hard. "Would you like to join me?"

"If Shechinah doesn't mind a double date with you, then I don't. Does She?"

Brandy stepped toward me, put her hands over mine, and told me to close my eyes as she closed hers. "Let's ask Her." With her lids seeming to flutter with a kind of concentration, she prayed, or feigned a little prayer or communion with the still sleeping— but soon to awaken—Jewish female forces.

Was this an act of irreverence or piety? It was hard to tell, but probably a walking of the line between the two. I walked along too, willingly, eagerly, blindly, while the corridor emptied except for us, and, I believe, Rabbi Greenwald, who was peering from beyond his half-closed classroom door. When Brandy saw him, she dropped my hands, terminated her prayer, and, leaving me standing there, said over her shoulder, "I don't think Shechinah minds at all. Pick me up at eight, She says. And don't be late, Jonah."

Brandy knew. She was choosing me. A sabbath date indeed. I am certain she saw the logic of it already. Like a line of Torah that clarifies a Talmudic puzzle, no matter that the Talmud was written thousands of years later. It is all connected and foreseen. All is predestined, even the illusion of free will. Brandy knew. She could see the beginning in the end and the end in the beginning. Like a ball of yarn.

And so our first date was made. Certainly I was happy to have been singled out—like Jonah, like all the biblical characters who were chosen. But the happiness that comes from being chosen is followed with irritating immediacy by the burden of distinction: the desire to flee not only today's responsibility, but also the future's. After all, when Moses was allowed to see the face of God on Sinai, was that not the high point of his life? But then, minutes later, he has to shlep the tablets down the mountain and somehow force those laws on a crowd of nomads dancing around the Golden Calf. The burden of it all! It's no wonder Michelangelo and Freud both have the lawgiver tearing his beard out with a vein-swollen hand and ready to dash the decalogue on the rocks. Perhaps we can save this material for the next meeting of the Men's Club. Do we have a Men's Club?

I had a date with Brandy! I went to the Greek's, on 123rd Street, and submitted myself to a scary razor cut. I bought a new tie. I skipped the deli and in general ate far less unkosher food for the remainder of the week. Studying up in my room with Big Lou, Arthur, and Ronnie, I tried to remain cool. I was cool. My friends helped me.

Let me tell you, beloved congregants, about my friends, my rabbinical pals. I'm proud of them. They were oddballs too and they made me feel not so alone. They were certainly not your run-of-the-mill studious rabbis-to-be, for I remember we spent far more time leafing through pages of girls than pages of Talmud. You have never suspected this rabbi of yours to have been, a long time ago, the leader of a small minyan of aspiring rabbinical ladies' men? Well, we love what we love.

So step forward, Big Lou, Arthur, and Ronnie, my old friends. Surface in my thoughts and settle beside Brandy Lee to present yourselves to my curious congregation. Considering how zipped up the Seminary was in the 1960s, our group and its comparatively modest and, to us, normal activity was perceived, we knew, as dangerous, potentially heretical, and in bad taste. All we did was dress a little defiantly, primarily by going tieless at services and wearing political buttons with occasional sexual messages. Was "Rabbis do it three times a day" one of them? Don't ask! Not on Yom Kippur. Another offense: we introduced girls in short skirts into the traditional sabbath meals at the Seminary dining room, and one of us—Big Lou, I believe—also publicly argued with Dr. Miles Rosenberg, the Seminary's slender resident ethicist, that sex before marriage would not bring down the wrath of the Almighty on a lonely rabbinical student. In short, we were always worried that Rabbi Greenwald and the other authorities would be on the phone to our parents. Now that I had somehow brought the superb Brandy Lee Wild Thing Snyder into our midst, she with her magnificent scholarly abilities and parentage, it was clear to some that I was hell-bent on corrupting one of the great daughters of Israel. How little they knew.

The others had the following traits and achievements of note: Big Lou, who was my roommate, was, despite his shortness, possessed of dark and handsome good looks that made it easy for him to find, pursue, and then unhappily date a succession of daughters of chief rabbis of small or exotic countries with minuscule Jewish populations, whose fathers happened to be in New York on religious sabbatical. Big Lou's dating curriculum vitae in the first years I knew him included Rena, the daughter of the chief rabbi of Scotland; Miriam Xiomara Shapira, daughter of the chief rabbi of Bolivia; and I believe the daughter of the chief rabbi of Rhodesia. After years of intensive therapy to break the daughters-of-chief-rabbis habit, Big Lou took a different tack and was at the time of our story dating Penelope, a Barnard art history major and friend of Brandy's. Penelope was barely a Jew at all, but the real problem was politics. She was a radical who had taken the Arab side in the 1967 War, and Lou had a hard time overlooking Penelope's challenging anti-Israel remarks. Uttered through Brigitte Bardot lips and a lovely smile, her attacks kept Lou continually on guard, and very interested. Plus she wasn't the daughter of a chief rabbi, or any rabbi. Lou found that immensely appealing and took the opportunity to warn me then about the pitfalls of dating daughters of chief rabbis, including chief rabbis of Kansas. He liked Brandy Lee and she him, but he knew whereof he spoke. I wish he had truly warned me.

Lou was the son of a Hebrew-school teacher from a small town in Vermont who no more knew why he was at the Seminary than I. One afternoon, fresh from a therapeutic insight, he told me his life had almost certainly taken its pattern from the fact that his father was the first American soldier to enter Tripoli, liberate the town, and in the euphoria of victory and of still being alive, promise his buddies to marry the first Jewish woman he saw. Enter Lou's mother, Babette, a short, olive-skinned beauty, whom he wed in 1945, with both Ike and Montgomery attending for the public relations value. She, of course, turned out to be the daughter of the chief rabbi of Tripoli.

. And what of the others I mentioned? Arthur was a searcher, a mystic from Miami, Florida, who loved the Grateful Dead and Cat Stevens, selections from whom he always played in his room while reading the Zohar and other Kabalistic texts. Arthur had fallen in love with Barbara, a beautiful, innocent young woman from Georgia who spoke in tongues and whose father handled snakes in the rural church back home. He told her about his interest in Jewish mysticism, and she was very much taken by it. The problem was Arthur never knew if she loved him or the Baal Shem Tov, whose tales he told her all the time.

Arthur's best friend and roommate, Ronnie, was a nervous wreck from Chicago; between the two of them there was one balanced personality. Ronnie, who daily tried to observe all 613 mitzvot, or commandments, was simply too anxious all the time to have a regular girlfriend, although he had an uncanny ability to find and date psychiatric nurses from the locked wards of local hospitals. There was something in their profoundly intent manner that he found very soothing.

On sabbath nights, when we had drunk enough sacramental wine, Big Lou, Arthur, Ronnie, and your rabbi-to-be joked that we were the Four Questions come to life out of the Passover Haggadah. We asked how and why we four rabbinical students were different from all other rabbinical students, and the answers we came up with were scary, bitter, and wanting. At the end of each sabbath, Arthur celebrated havdolah, the return of the regular week, by inviting us and whoever our girlfriends were at the time to join him in a circle on the floor of his room. There we sat and read aloud from Buber's *Tales of the Hasidim*, while he cut up his cube of LSD and offered each of us a flake with a slug of orange juice. After we finished Buber, we moved on to Aldous Huxley, whose *Gates of Perception* provided me my first mystical experience and motivated me to try translating it into Hebrew.   Later we found the Lurias and the Luzzato mystics of Safed to join us on our trips and, in some fashion, to put the rabbinical seal of approval on them. It was a new and beautiful Jewish ceremony, Arthur insisted, but since you could get five to fifteen for this particular hallucinogenic ritual, we locked the door and barricaded it with a bookcase.

Ronnie's particular contribution to our rabbinical peace of mind was that he was an expert at how to sever the jugular veins of various quadrupeds. He had been considering following his father's vocation of ritual slaughterer, and, on graduation, starting a training institute to revive interest among young Jews in the profession. After his first trip on Arthur's acid, however, he was no longer confident that he could brush his teeth, let alone hold the slaughterer's knife, or even become a rabbi.

We Questions were neither wise nor wicked; we just didn't know what the hell was going on most of the time. We had some cynicism, to be sure, but also we were genuine searchers in a place with little toleration for it. We would have been less stigmatized had we been gifted students like Brandy, or geniuses, which in the view of our elders would have made our questioning challenging and profound instead of merely irritating.

We began to take bets on who would drop out first. But somehow we studied well enough together to pass tests and still found time, just as Rabbi Greenwald had accused, to organize the rent strikes, to work for Students for a Democratic Society at Columbia, to prepare for the takeover there, and, in general, to try to tear the place down. The Seminary, however, did not lend itself to tearing down. Nor did we want to, although eventually Rabbi Greenwald was convinced we might become a danger to the institution. That is why, I am certain, he tormented us, especially your rabbi-to-be, with impossibly difficult assignments. I skipped class as much as I could.

But I need to tell you about my first date with Brandy Lee, my dear congregants, possible Rabbinical Search Committee members soon to be meeting, my Jews, my weekend monks of the yellow robe, my Tibetan specialists, my friends. For days I had found myself absorbed by the desire to study and to excel more than I ever had in my years at the Seminary. I was a young scholar on fire. At times with Big Lou, at times with Arthur, sometimes even alone, I studied. Brandy Lee inspired me. I wanted to do well, to make her proud, especially in front of Rabbi Greenwald, in whose class we would sit two more times before the blessed sabbath of that first date arrived. During those sessions I vowed to show Brandy I had the right stuff to take him on. When my turn came, I muffed the question, and received Rabbi Greenwald's ridicule; yet Brandy knew I had risked—and endured—humiliation for her. When the ordeal was over, her quick glance at me said, I will make it up to you, I will comfort you, wait for the sabbath.

What was the venue for this historical date, you ask, oh listeners to your rabbi's Torah, to his journey up from the fish's belly? Where would we go after services? But the question is moot! Where else would a rabbinical student, even your renegade rogue rabbi, bring a date, especially Brandy Lee, the premier Kansas Talmudist of the younger generation, on shabbos. It is the day of rest, my congregants. It is a time to remind ourselves that there *is* no time except the human grid we place on the morning and the evening, the first day. And then, after six, we rest. So do we go to the movies? One doesn't carry money. For a drive? Get real! One doesn't ignite engines. For a walk along the Hudson? One doesn't want one's date to be mugged and one's own stupid young clerical throat cut.

We went to the Seminary dining room.

But first I had to pick up Brandy Lee under the lights at the iron gates of Barnard College. When I arrived exactly at the appointed time, she was not there. I waited for ten minutes. I watched a dozen couples pass me, turning downtown, toward Greenwich Village, the folk concerts, the jazz, the *Figaro* and the latest Bergman film, toward all the fine non-shabbos action of New York that I yearned for and rejected in equal measure.

Was it possible I was being stood up? I decided to go into the dormitory to phone Brandy when from the dark copse near where I stood, I heard a rustling. This is how I remember it, dear friends who, like me, suffer from desire and craving. A profound and tantalizing rustling, and then out of the shadows from behind the shrubs and into the lamplight she stepped. Her hair was pulled up into a French braid in the back, tied by a white band. There were not one but three Israeli turquoise combs in her hair, and right in the center, dangling over the hair line, was a gleaming green gem. Like a movie star in the first days of film, being introduced inside an ever-nearing illuminated cameo, she approached. Her perfect figure was set off by a white dress that was tight at the waist, with buttons up from the fountain of the mysterious omphalos toward the neckline. At the juncture where the chest divided into separate breasts, Brandy's gold Star of David relaxed in its small fossa and gleamed with the reflected light of the lamps on Broadway. Her alligator boots came up calf-high, and over the right one she wore a red bandana pulled tight like a garter.

"That's where I carry my keys," she said, when she caught me staring, "so I don't have to carry on the sabbath. You know."

Did I ever! In a kind of regal gesture Brandy offered her hand to me. When I took it, she turned herself slowly around, to the polite applause of two or three guys who, with their dates, were walking out toward Broadway.

Witnesses of my falling in love, my seduction, my wisdom and folly!

Then she said, "Your Sabbath Queen has arrived." I felt my pupils dilate in the darkness. I had the unusual experience of being speechless. I answered by bowing slightly, as I often do now. I love bowing, it comes quite naturally, my congregants. I love to get down low on the ground, near to the dead. Did not Buddha himself—no comparison intended—see, upon leaving the refuge of his father's palace, a sick person and a corpse, both on the ground? Has someone given some analysis to this inclination of your rabbi? We are the most bowing congregation in America, and I am proud of you.

Brandy returned the bow and said, "Arise, young rabbi, and tell me why you are here."

Nonplussed by her, as always, I answered, "I got here twenty minutes ago. Where were you? Why were you hiding?"

"I wasn't hiding. You were! I've been reading for Medieval English Romance all week and I want to talk this way; it's fun. Now play along," she commanded, "and tell me, what country are we traveling to, my knight, I mean my young rabbi?"

"We're traveling to Seminaryland, Brandy. A dangerous place, where teacher-monsters lie in wait and twist tender ears off innocents to embarrass them."

"I will protect you," she declared. "What other dangers lurk?"

"Large books fall off shelves and hit you both day and night. It's a land where the search is everything and where a correct answer is only a clue in the never-ending quest. The goal is unclear but the journey goes on forever. How am I doing?"

She looked into my eyes briefly and then away. "My knight," she whispered, and then she turned, took my hand, and began to lead us north, to Seminaryland. I smelled her by-now-familiar perfume, and then several new scents announced themselves: the crispness of her facial cream, the sunny, outdoor scent of her just-laundered clothing, the herbal conditioner in her hair. I felt, as we walked north to Seminaryland, that I was indeed being drawn in for the first time to the wonderful new land of exotic women's cosmetics, a land over which Brandy was the undisputed queen. As the sidewalk dipped and the crenelated tower of the Seminary loomed into view, with its Burning Bush emblazoned beneath the upper window, we paused. Brandy drew my face down to hers. "Are you afraid, young rabbi?"

"The Sabbath Queen is my friend; she's always by my side. I'm not afraid."

"I will stay by your side tonight, too, and, if you play your cards right, for many nights to come."

"I hardly know you."

"I'm an open book," she whispered.

I drew in a long deep breath, exhaled, and tried to calm myself through focusing on the minute place at the end of the nostrils where the breath passes as it leaves and reenters the body. I said, "Don't I first have to win you over? Isn't that part of the script? Aren't you going to present me with a mission?"

"Like Jonah?" she said.

"Yes," I answered, with a tremble. "I need to accomplish great deeds."

"Magnificent deeds," she said. We crossed Broadway in front of a huge, noisy truck. We walked up the steps into campus, past the security guard, beneath the Burning Bush. "Yes, you must perform heroic labors," she whispered, "though they need not be intellectual; the details can be worked out later." We stepped to the side, around the corner from the

Education Building, and she stood next to me, very close, so that I felt her points and curves, her woman's full geometry against my shirt. She looked deep into my eyes and asked, "Do you find me too strange? Some people do."

Oh, my congregants, a spell had been cast, a great Jewish spell, and was I ever caught in it! "I find you fascinating," I said, "beyond my poor ability to describe." We could smell the fried chicken and the broccoli and the hot prune pudding wafting toward us from the well-lighted Seminary dining room across the arcade. I much preferred Brandy's various scents and hoped for a wind change. "You're without a doubt one of the most interesting people I have ever met. Maybe *the* most interesting."

In retrospect, I believe these remarks disappointed her with their banality. Nevertheless, she answered, "I hardly know you, too, and yet I feel like praying with you. Prayer is very intimate, and I feel I want to pray with no one else but Jonah Grief tonight. Let us pray, young rabbi. Just you, I, and the Sabbath Queen, alone yet together tonight."

"It is good," I said, rising to the occasion—thank God—"that the Sabbath Queen is in such a mood tonight. Her subjects adore her and await her for the start of evening prayers."

That was when Brandy slipped her hand under my jacket, circled my waist, and slowly fanned out her fingers until they came to rest across my ribs. That is how we traversed the Seminary's quadrangle. One of the most exciting ambles of your rabbi's entire life. We entered the Education Building like this, together as a unit, and heard the sweet and yearning sounds of the service drift up to welcome us from the chapel below.

Would it be accurate to say that for me, at that time and in that place, Brandy Lee was a kind of prayer answered? Only in the colloquial sense, for the verb, to pray, in Hebrew, is always reflexive. It is not asking God for health, long life, protection from pogroms, sexual relief, or a load of other benefits. No, prayer is pure self-examination and excruciating self-judgment. Perhaps what Brandy saw in me those many years ago was my endless ability to examine and question motives and sincerity, and with what uncommon talent and punctuality I point out our failings.

And yet when I entered the small synagogue room beneath the Seminary with Brandy Lee, on my lips was a prayer as conventional and trashy as if I had copied it out of an adolescent movie-star magazine, only in Hebrew: Hear oh Israel, the Lord our God, the Lord is One, it said. Please, please, make what is happening between me and Brandy real! Don't let me discover that it is pure illusion. Who would have thought that such an incredible girl would like me? If you do this for me, Lord, I said, in return I will find many new ways to worship you. If you see to it that she stays with me, then I will study harder, I will forego the cheeseburgers and the secret Chinese sweet and sour pork lunch specials, $1.95. I will become a good rabbi. I will stop making fun of my elders. I will not omit a single word of the Eighteen Benedictions, the Shmoney Esray. I will worship you with new sincerity all the days of my life, and it will not be that which has been taught and given to me secondhand; it will not be trying to locate radical amazement in my life, the mysterium tremendum in the sands of the seas and stars of heaven. I will discover, Lord, something genuinely of my own and build upon it a new rock for Israel.

You see that even in my zealousness at that rich, emotional, and prayerful moment with Brandy Lee, the form my prayer took was nevertheless the If-I-Do-This, Then-Please-Do-That, the Let's-Make-a-Deal school of prayer. Yet perhaps Brandy saw beyond, saw the beginning in the end and the end in the beginning. Perhaps she had a sense of the full circle of life, as I have mentioned. From the instant I laid eyes on Brandy Lee, I felt myself drowning in her sea and going deeper and deeper all the time. Enjoying myself now and then, to be sure, but a sinking feeling was right there at the very beginning, and in the very center of my love for her.

Brandy Lee surely must have had her doubts about me, her late-night hesitations after we kissed and went back each of us to our rooms. She must have sensed how poorly her expectations matched the person I was. She was an original all right. However, more painful to her than her gradually growing disappointment in me must have also been—again, courtesy of me—the troubling self-revelation that her need for attention was bottomless and I certainly couldn't satisfy it. Thus her clothes, her extreme stylishness, her drama, her panache.

The fact that I, her soon-to-be boyfriend and then husband, was the harbinger of such insights— and that they took the form of telling her she was the greatest tease in all Israel—should have made her doubt our prospects. With our higher awareness still imprisoned and in darkness because of our traditional upbringing and religion, with our spirit still unlighted by meditation and not yet set free, our egos ran rampant. She showed no hesitation, and neither did I. In a phrase, we were impulsive idiots in love.

We fell into a publicly subdued but intense courtship, to the envy, I believe, of Rabbi Greenwald, and the consternation of our soon-to-be united families, who were told little about it until the end. Big Lou, Ronnie, and Arthur serenaded Brandy and me in my Seminary room with great cantorial moments on the ukelele. We double- and triple-dated on Sunday nights on Macdougal Street, taking in Judy Collins, the Smothers Brothers, and the San Francisco Mime Troupe in a benefit for the Black Panthers. We studied together at Barnard, where I was introduced to Ada and Lea, Brandy's pre-med roommates. I joked and carried books for my beloved. We became a couple.

And yet we had a big problem, which we at first called a virtue. For I was a young rabbi-to-be and

Brandy was a young daughter of rabbis and a future wife of a rabbi, and surely God had commanded us to know each other. And if two people at the Seminary studying Talmud and Torah and drawn madly to each other's bodies in the great and tumultuous bed-hopping summers of 1968, 1969, and even 1970 can not know each other in the biblical sense, then, my lovely children of Israel, who can?

You see, for many a night after the initiatory sabbath date I have described—yea, for months— the dating scenario went, more or less, like this: Return with Brandy, fifteen minutes before the midnight curfew, to the "living room" of the Barnard dorms (later, after her graduation, the venue would change to Brandy's various apartments around the Upper West Side, but not the general scenario) to our necking spot on the faded white sofa in the corner. Look deeply into Brandy's green eyes while making a witty remark about the old-fashioned puritanical antimacassars. Begin to run fingers through the thickets of her wild red hair. Become intimate with her various facial creams, inhale their fascinating and ever-changing flavors, joke nervously that I could catalog them biblically—frankincense, myrrh, thyme. Dive into the depressions behind her ears, on the slope of her neck where the perfume concentrated and pooled. Revisit the spot on her clavicle where if my mouth lingered long enough, she would go crazy.

At times we began to kiss so much, it turned to a kind of biting and clawing, my fish and I. Then Wild Thing, vomiting out all modesty, opened her mouth to me. In Jonah dove, like a trapeze artist who no longer cares if there's a net below. Oh how fit I was to burst, and did, alone, later, because Brandy, a young voluptuous orthodox woman, had her standards and I, a young rabbi-to-be, had mine.

And yet it seemed to me, in the midst of my heady joy and good luck, also remarkably sad, for the rest of the world, I was certain, was wildly consummating their love, in quiet mockery of us. All the while we fought to uphold our moral code—that is, masturbated—the rest of our generation, with perhaps the exception of our equally noble and onanistic counterparts at the Protestant and Catholic seminaries, were all coupling away in their beds, on mattresses in the park, on the seats of cars, in delivery vans stuck in rush hour, on stairwells, on the floors of family rooms vacated by parents, behind thick drapes, in the cabins of summer camps, in the upstairs rooms of social clubs, at SDS meetings while the ditto machine's rattle conceals the squeal of orgasms, in hotels, elevators, basements, in closets, train compartments, in the bathrooms of 747s while lines form impatiently outside, on the branches of old tree houses, on carpets beside winter fires, on the sands of beaches, as God and nature have commanded.

But we devoured one another only within the limits I describe until the proctor tapped me on the shoulder saying, "The dorm is closed to visitors, young man." Yes, Brandy and I saved ourselves for each other and for Israel all the days of our dating and engagement—yea for three and a half years! Amen.

Brandy Lee's stunning beauty, her world-class coquetry, and her fine brain, as if Sarah Bernhardt and Moses Maimonides' somehow were fused into one exquisite human, were so powerful that a person with my own relatively poor endowments could not possibly resist. As determining as anything else, I suppose, was Brandy's inexplicable enthusiasm for my miserable carcass and central nervous system, a power that seemed to sweep away all doubts and make our decision okay. We suffered, we endured, we persevered through sexual abstinence. A learning experience for your rabbi, and far more; for, as a result, we felt we were embarked on a great adventure.

Months went by, then a full year, as the sexual clock ticked away, and still we didn't know each other. We weren't exactly ignorant of each other, of course. In time we became naked to the waist with each other. On one or two memorable nights we were even naked to the underwear with each other, too. I, in my blue boxers and Brandy in her —nope, I won't dwell on it except to say she wore Lily de France and I Fruit of the Loom. Yet we had evolved an unwritten pact: We could stop, and we would! We could douse the passion no matter how fiery it grew.

Couldn't we?

Was this extended abstinence the right choice for us? Today, my congregants, in the era of AIDS and many other sexually transmitted diseases, I say that it was. On the other hand, never forget that Buddha achieved his enlightenment not from abstinence but only when he gave up his long fast and asceticism and began to make love.

Have I answered your question about abstinence? Have you asked one, my beloved congregation of ventriloquists? You, who speak, God help me, so often in my own voice. Yes, of course, Brandy and I were able to maintain a standard precisely because we knew we were going to marry. About that there was soon a growing conviction that admitted few hesitations or questions.

Brandy and I were by now a major couple, known, followed, and envied throughout Seminary-land and somewhat beyond. We were semipublic figures, with attendant responsibilities. Big Lou and Penelope, Arthur and Barbara, and many other rabbinical couples-in-formation followed our moves. Couples struggling for a relationship that expressed not political or even emerging feminist but religious values emulated us. Masturbators eyed us from their lonely windowsills. How foolish and blind is the world! And we walked so insouciantly through it all, through campus demonstrations and fraternity parties, through rent strikes and prayer vigils, past the Tactical Patrol Force with their truncheons, and past handsomely bearded Rabbi

Finkelstein leaning on his elegant cane as he waited at a traffic light on his way home from services.

We went everywhere hand in hand, sharing fried chicken dinner every sabbath in the Seminary dining room, chanting together the birkat hamazon, the beautiful grace after meals, shoulder to shoulder, neck to neck, two cantillating Jewish lovebirds. We prayed, we studied, and she saved me in Talmud class, intermediate and advanced. In April, when I had my most serious religious crisis and told her I no longer thought I believed in God, Brandy put her beautifully manicured hands on my shoulders, squared me to her, and said with quiet conviction, "You will, I promise."

After she rescued me religiously, we came close to living together. But since we were not married, and, since we were not yet sleeping together, what was the point? So our values were threatened, but somehow they held and we felt closer to each other than ever before. We heard and were not embarrassed by each other's trickle and fart behind the unlocked bathroom door. We were a number, we were milk and honey, we were destined.

On a Thursday afternoon, a month before ordination, some fifty-seven hundred years since the creation of the world, my proud parents flew in from Los Angeles for the wedding; Brandy's extended family touched down on a specially chartered rabbinical jet from Kansas. My mother was thrilled by the upcoming event and by the

Seminary, for which she and Rabbi Hall's sisterhood had been raising money for years. To Edith, arrival at the Seminary, cradle of the Conservative Movement, headquarters of the founder Solomon Schechter and Mrs. Schechter, was a kind of coming home, a return to an American Jerusalem; continuing on to the Land of Israel would be entirely unnecessary. To Edith, this was Junior Cong grown up.

As always, my father behaved, well, less than admirably. When Mo saw all the rabbis, young, middle-aged, and ancient—easily five percent of the Rabbinical Assembly, Midwest division—and when they, in particular, began to ask him for details about his education and business background, he was inspired immediately to phone the Atlantic City Visitors' Bureau, through whom he located a great deal—three days and two nights at the Grand Diamond Hotel, including round-trip bus fare, for $29.95.

The two families had little in common, of course, except the apparent passionate love shared by their respective offspring. But there was soon something more, a strange soufflé of suspicion, and a hope began to grow as family members shook hands and began to share prenuptial breakfasts and teas together. That is, as soon as they began talking. Our impulsive, crazy children have gone off and done something stupid—so the suspicion and hope silently expressed themselves in the celebrants' minds, although they remained largely invisible to bride and groom. Somehow, they thought, would it not be better for everyone concerned, including those responsible for the future of Jewish life in the United States, to abort this simcha, this about-to-happen joyous event, before it becomes a fact?

Rabbi Greenwald had decided, you see, to give a party in honor of the wedding of his greatest student, Wild Thing, to perhaps his worst, me. It actually was a wonderful if surprising gesture on Greenwald's part, and the place was really hopping—the rabbis, Big Lou and Arthur singing duets of Hebrew and Yiddish songs, Ronnie, Lea, and Ada. But several times that evening I saw my father go in and out of the bedroom with Brandy's venerable dad and other members of the Snyder clan, all looking somber and worried. The rabbis reemerged wearing solemn faces, shaking their heads, and muttering. Something told me not to ask what was going on, and I concentrated instead on squiring my mother about the room and making introductions.

Edith, dazzled by all these greats of Israel, eventually fainted. She was revived in the kitchen by Wild Thing's grandmother, the only bobbe I ever saw before or since wearing tasteful diamonds and a Stetson, and by Rabbi Greenwald's wife. When it came time for a practice run of the traditional lifting of bride and groom aloft on people's shoulders, I noticed a sudden odd reluctance of the Midwesterners to participate, as if they knew something we did not. Add to that my father's checking the time on his watch as if he still hoped he might make the Atlantic City bus late that night.

Okay, my conspiratorial congregants, Kabalists and cabal-ists, here's what I think unfolded: In my opinion the Snyders approached Dad first with a deal they thought a character like him couldn't refuse. According to this deal, he would promise to talk me out of the marriage in exchange for a nice piece of change. They expected Dad to be so mercenary that it would become only a question of haggling about the amount. A kind of reverse dowry, a substitute for the bride. I expect they rightly may have been confident of success with Mo, but the rabbis didn't figure Edith into the equation. The Snyders never counted on Edith Grief's pride, her honor, and her inordinate, all-encompassing, insatiable love of rabbis, even, apparently, dishonorable ones who did not appreciate her son's specialness and suspected me of compensating for my own poor abilities by becoming a kind of rabbinical gold digger. When Mo told her what they had proposed— and there was no way he could avoid telling her and expect to live to see another horse race or eat another spoonful of chicken soup—she fainted.

By the time she revived, a sea change had occurred. She ceased speaking to the Snyders and to my father—except for the most perfunctory hello, good-bye, good night, mazel tov, thank you for the smelling salts—and the party was soon over.

The marriage ceremony to follow was, as you will soon hear, quite peculiar, but it took place.

I remember it all now as if it had occurred just this morning. That is why I am about to make a toast with this bottle of sabbath wine, most of which I have just polished off. Blessed art Thou oh Lord our God, King of the Universe, Who has created the fruit of the vine!

Well, we are once again in the below-ground chapel of the Seminary, the clogged, stressed, and occasionally happy scene of the Snyder-Grief nuptial extravaganza. Big Lou and Arthur are standing at opposite ends of the old dais with its unstable iron railing. My best men, they are gently rocking back and forth while chanting melodies derived from the most erotic passages of Psalms: luscious red lips dripping honey and myrrh, loves that await me in the valley of Sharon, where the hills race like young rams and the Jordan floods its banks. Wild Thing-inspired ideas. My friends have stayed up a good part of the night practicing, and their renderings, although highly unorthodox, are beautiful, and in their own way respectful of tradition.

Over by the door is the last of the Four Questions, Ronnie, my chief and only usher, who, as it will turn out, will be the next of us to marry. He already has begun to sweat, a mustache of droplets on his narrow face that today more than ever reminds me of a smiling, good-hearted young goat. He is in constant motion, ululating along with Arthur and Big Lou, handing out yarmulkes and prayer shawls, shaking hands, saying mazel tov to Brandy's family, the leaders of Midwestern Jewry, in the hope—this is our design—that six months from now, one of them might remember Ronnie and offer him an assistant rabbi's job or maybe, mirabile dictu, a pulpit of his own.

Brandy is wearing Great Bobbe Ruth's splendid white wedding dress, an acre of tulle, muslin, rare calico, and other fabrics of the Ohio Valley wound about her, a family heirloom and an article lovingly and immaculately preserved from the pioneer Jewish peddling days on the Kansas frontier. The diaphanous brocade rises from her cleavage toward her chin, where it separates into a v high on her neck. There, the new gold Star of David I have given her sits like a lovely beacon. Her cowboy boots, Krylonned white for the occasion, are visible beneath the voluminous hem of the gown. Although it is beyond hopeless for me to even try to match her, Brandy has canvassed one dozen Manhattan antique clothing stores and finally found a white 1940s tuxedo of the kind Fred Astaire might have worn to his bar mitzvah. It is a little tight but, good sport that I am, I have stuffed myself in. A shirt to match, with French front, makes me feel as if my life has suddenly catapulted me to the top of an immense wedding cake. If I bend over too far, something will surely rip, or, perhaps better, I will topple off.

I remember my wedding ceremony in 1972 as I do a page of Talmud, badly and in a nervous haze. Brandy's parents are huddling somewhere before we begin. In the dim light falling from the transom I can see the tears welling up in her father's gray eyes. His wife, with whom I've barely spoken a word, is clinging to his arm, feeling, I can only imagine, what a wonderful institution marriage is but, in the same instant, what an oaf I must be, the highly undistinguished—they have spoken, I know, at length with Rabbi Greenwald!—instrument separating her prosperous, loving parents from Wild Thing.

My own progenitors, as always, are hard to find. Do they ever make it to their assigned places in the first rows? Like me today, they appear to be trying to do the impossible: hide. I finally locate Edith's expectant and hopeful face. After the intrigue and fainting of the previous night, I know that her public expression conceals shame and anger and that immediately after the ceremony she expects me to get her to the airport. I offer her the best smile I can muster.

As for my father, who stands beside her, his face is extremely lively and animated. I don't understand this until I hear the sudden crackle of a transistor radio turned up and then instantly silenced in response to an enraged wave of hushing. Mo has become addicted to radio talk shows, especially those dealing with religion, and when he can't go to gamble or to the track, he goes to the radio, arguing aloud with the hosts and pointing out the prejudices of the callers. The thoughtlessness of this at his son's wedding here in the heart of the Seminary chapel, profoundly offending some of the world's greatest Judaic scholars, is hard to understand, or forgive.

And yet how well I understand now. If you think we are beneath you, he seems to be saying, I'll give you folks an earful! It was his version of a parental gesture: to rabbis, priests, and ministers invisible on the air, he is combative, but in person he is a pussy cat. Has the apple fallen far from the tree, my friends? Up on this pulpit I am full of Jewish sound and fury, and Buddhist teaching also rolls easily from my lips. But in person, one to one, I have only recently come into my own. Thank God Arthur and Big Lou sing louder than ever, drowning out the few blasting seconds of *Religion on the Line* or whatever Mo is trying to listen to. My mother grabs the radio concealed in his pocket and rips out the batteries. I remember vowing—for the tenth or eleventh time in my life—never to speak to him again.

Of the brief walk up to the dais I recall the appraising and disapproving eyes boring in on me left and right, and from behind, in particular, Brandy's father's eyes. However, I know that Brandy, by his side now, perfumed and rustling, will soon be beside me. Then I will whisper to her the two worries overwhelming me: namely, that my antique trousers are about to rip apart in their antique seat, and also that what we are about to do is a grave mistake.

"Pull in those buns, darling," she said, "and please try to smile a little? Just for me?"

When we arrived at the dais, Rabbi Shalom Joshua was waiting for us, with his strong hands holding the prayer book over his heart. He is the dean of the Rabbinical School, a renowned and widely published Jewish philosopher and Kabalist who is also Arthur's hero and role model. Rabbi Joshua is a vigorous, broad-shouldered, and handsome man, a teacher whose courses I have always shunned out of fear of disappointing him and discovering that my academic failings extend beyond Talmud, deep into the heart of Jewish spirituality as well. For he is one of those charismatic, white-bearded scholars on my mother's Mt. Sinai Mortuary calendar, whose noble and sparkling-eyed visage hints at the forbidden-to-look-upon face of God.

Rabbi Joshua's agreeing to marry Brandy and me is a great honor, which came to us not only because Arthur has asked him for a special favor, but also clearly because Wild Thing's family is so distinguished. And there is another less visible but far more important reason, which Arthur has revealed to me: Rabbi Joshua senses some special spirituality in our union—perhaps the Kabalistic significance of the uniting of opposites: the c-minus male and the splendid, genius female.

So the melodies are chanted, the sniffles are heard, the readings are read, and then Rabbi Joshua asks Brandy and me each to repeat, in turn, Haray at mikudesh et lee b'taba-at zu: Behold you are holy and set aside for me, you are blessed with this ring in the eyes of God and Israel, and by the power vested in me by the city and state of New York . . .

And it was over, almost.

All but the breaking of the glass. I raised my rabbinical foot high above the white package and I was ready to crush the little bastard to bits all safely wrapped in its thick cloth napkin. I didn' t even care if I ripped my agonizingly tight antique pants in the process. But I hesitated. I waited two, then three seconds, my sole hovering over the target, a World War II film actor, suspended; I have braved the flak but at the critical moment my bomb-bay doors suddenly jam. Five seconds, ten, a major hiatus. This is a fact. Ask Big Lou. Ask the others of the Four Questions wherever they are. I held, I froze.

The purpose of the breaking of the glass, as you may know, my friends and autodidacts of the Tuesday morning current events group, is, according to a medieval folk tradition, to frighten away devils who hover about happy occasions and ruin them if they can. According to an older, rabbinical, and far less amusing source, we are charged, through the sound of breaking glass, to remember tears, wailing, and havoc, as might have occurred at the holy temple's two destructions, the expulsions from Egypt, Spain, France, England, the York massacre, the Chelmnietski pogroms, and of course Kristallnacht and all that came after, thus maintaining the famous Jewish habit of never keeping sorrow too far afield from joy.

But that glass held yet another more personal meaning for me. I felt close to that glass, as if I were actually in it; as if it might be a cozy little glass house and I the tiny yarmulked homunculus living within its cool, smooth walls. As the seconds ticked away, as rabbis and parents and teachers held their breath in the silence, I kept refusing to give in and provide the swift, dramatic crack that would show how decisive, powerfully hoofed, and emphatic I could be, a demonstration of Jewish machismo! No, I would not be one to play into that script. For I felt I really was in that little glass house, and how, therefore, could I be expected to stomp myself to smithereens? That we humans often spend our lives doing this in so many other ways was not yet obvious to me.

When the embarrassment of Rabbi Joshua and the others became palpable, I lowered my foot, finally coming gently and harmlessly to rest on the glass.

I hoped, of course, in my immature and boyish heart, that rings and brachot and ceremonies notwithstanding, if I simply did not break the glass, if we could just skip this one gesture with its noisy finality and keep the pocketed fingers of one hand crossed, then the ceremony would somehow not be truly valid and official.

I felt dizzy and upside down, still suspended. I must have known the marriage was a big mistake, and yet had it not already gone way beyond my power to stop? Why hadn't the Kansas rabbis pressured Brandy? What in the world did she continue to see in yours truly? While I teetered on the glass, somebody even joked that I was reenacting the famous story of how Rabbi Hillel had taught the essence of Torah to a busy man who had asked that

Hillel convey the lesson in a hurry, in the time a man could remain standing on one foot.

Brandy began to pull on my arm. "Enough's enough," she whispered. I knew she wanted me to look at her, because it is out of those deep brown eyes, those windows to her soul, that her authority and command over me radiated. I avoided them.

Keeping my own eyes fixed on the glass, I finally said, "Brandy, you want to just run out of here? Forget the marriage? Stay good friends forever?"

She chucked me firmly on the chin, cupped my face in her hand, and turned me toward her as if I were a child. And was I not? And are we all not, some smarter, some dumb, some well behaved and some violent, we children of Israel?

"How could such a thought even enter your head, Jonah?"

What I saw in her eyes then was precisely what I feared, the look that would pervade the balance of our marriage: a molten dark glow made of equal parts incredibly high hopes, torrid and kinky passion, and already smoldering frustration. As it is written, chapter 2, verse six:

The waters compassed me about, even to the soul
The deep was round about me.
The weeds were wrapped about my head.

"Pay attention," she suddenly ordered, "and follow me." Brandy then raised her awesome boot, with its brightly capped silver toe peeking out from the hem of her dress. With her ineluctable will and panache, she had found a way out. Instantly I understood what she would have me do.

"Achat, shtayim, shalosh," we called out together in Hebrew. "One, two, three!" Then the two of us, she in the most expensive boots Neiman Marcus had ever sold and I in my $12.50 Thom McCann loafers, drew up and descended as a team on that poor glass, crushing it with a great shattering.

A sudden peal of laughter and a loud murmur of relief rolled mercifully across the room. Arthur and Big Lou struck up a medley that included a klezmer version of "(I Can't Get No) Satisfaction." Mazel tovs and l'chayims abounded, and there was even talk of how Brandy and I had created, planned, and demonstrated this variation on the Jewish marriage ceremony, even including the dramatic flamingo leg hold that had preceded it. Why? In order, of course, to insert a new egalitarian gesture into the ritual, one that was certain to appeal to bright, young, forward-thinking women, a gesture soon to be adopted in progressive marriage ceremonies of the Conservative Jewish movement all across America.

Have I delayed long enough? Not quite. I would like to summon counselors and scholars other than myself to sit in and explain the failure of my marriage. I would request the experts be summoned immediately. Please step forward as I call your names: the Gaon of Vilna, the Magid of Meserich, the Lion of Judah, the Sigmund of Freud, the Ruth of Westheimer, the Duke of Earl. Speak up now! But first, join my congregants—and me, of course —in a glass: Blessed art Thou O Lord our God, King of the Universe, Who has created the fruit of the vine. How I love that blessing! We're getting quite close now. I assure you. If you therefore will all turn with me to our text, you will see that as Jonah dropped head over heels down through the waters, he called out to the Lord, as it is written:

I went down to the bottoms of the mountains
The earth and her bars closed upon me forever
Yet hast Thou brought up my life from the pit,
O Lord my God.

Thus did our prophet, with great accuracy, foretell the essence of my marriage to Wild Thing. The operative word is, of course, pit. Shachat in Hebrew, the root has connotations of the grave and even a particularly gruesome process of getting there—slaughter.

The pit, the dead place in your rabbi's marriage, dear congregants and amateur sexologists, was in what I—and, I am certain, Wild Thing—experienced as the deepest part, the nether world of our bodies. And it is there where this typical scene from early in the marriage occurred:

"Do you think I'm pretty?" Brandy asked as she sat on the stool before her vanity. Her clothes lay on the floor—as she loved nakedness almost as much as dressing up, her clothes were almost always on the floor within minutes of her return home. Now all she had on were the panties I had bought for her at the Spanish discount store. They were an acrylic material, I admitted, not terrifically pleasant to the touch, but we both liked the tulip-shaped flaps that adorned the front and back. She sat there brushing her thick hair, which in the early winter afternoon light shined with dramatic color contrasts. "You do think I'm pretty, don't you?"

"I happen to think you are the prettiest maid in all of Israel. Comely of form," I said, trying to remember lines from the Song of Songs and from Psalms. "Cheeks the color of the pomegranate, lips like new wine."

"Do you really think so?"

"If I were King David and needed someone to warm me, I would pick you every time. My Shulamit." The biblical stuff always turned her on. Needless to say, it came to both of us quite easily, and so our attempts at love-making were always laced with this hot erudition.

Brandy stood up and ran her hands down the sides of her body. "Shapely of breast and thigh, you think?"

"You bet," I answered. "Very shapely."

She took two little balletic leaps, landing in an arabesque position, which made her naked breasts jog and bob before they settled back into their accustomed places. I had nicknamed them Esther and Deborah, after heroines of Jewish history. In the same peculiar spirit, she had a few names for me and my parts too. She seemed to want to hear more. "Your hills race like young rams," I said. "You undulate like the waves of the Jordan."

"Then why won't you look at me?" she said, suddenly very bold.

"I do," I told her. "I look at you all the time."

It was her turn to avert her eyes now, but not before she gave me a glance fraught with skepticism and pity. She peered into her mirror. She could see me in the mirror now too, looking at her body, she looking back at me, at my reaction not so much to her body but to looking at her body in the glass. It was complicated, it was one big Gordian knot of reflection, judgment, reflection. Suddenly throwing back her shoulders, Brandy said almost in a shout, "Is it true you have sent your messengers throughout the land?"

"Yes, it is. I have sent them everywhere, and it is always the same," I assured her. "They never come back with anyone lovelier than you!"

"Then perhaps the problem is, Jonah," she said, "that you are playing the part of an old, old king. Is that what makes you act old, my old King David?"

What she referred to, no doubt, was my evident lack of arousal in the face of all this stimulation. It was only that too much stimulation, like too much Talmud, had led to diminishing returns. "I am not acting old," I lied.

"My panties are on. Should I put my bra on too?"

"You're fine as you are."

She peered down at my crotch. In my boxers there was, alas, still not the slightest bulge. "Perhaps you did not search diligently enough throughout the land, my king." She chortled, or laughed, or giggled in a voice I found very disturbing. Then she touched her index finger to her tongue. She wetted her nipple with the finger and, holding it aloft, came over to the edge of the bed where I was seated. "Did you send your messengers from Dan in the north to Beersheba in the south?"

"I did."

"To the mountains and the valleys?"

"Yes."

Now she took my finger, placed it in her mouth, and, extracting it, guided me in wetting the second nipple. "You see what feels good?"

"I see, Brandy."

"From the Jordan to the sea?"

"They were sent," I said, "by camel and horse as fast as they could go." She placed her arm over my shoulders, her face near mine. "Everywhere my chamberlains ordered beauty contests throughout the land to see who would sleep with the king to warm him."

"And I have won?" she whispered, as her hand moved from my midsection down to the elastic of my boxers.

Her body smelled very good, a Jewish perfume of bsomim, the spices frankincense and myrrh that sweetly usher out the sabbath and introduce the week to come; her skin was warm, pliant, and fair as the wax of a white candle. She was working hard, oh so hard, and I knew it. "You win," I yelled. "You have won the goddam beauty contest!"

"And what is it I have won?" she asked, bolting from the bed. "The right to sleep with the two-thousand-year-old man?"

"I've never concealed from you that I have a self-image problem."

"You joke about it," she answered, "but this is no joke. We've waited for so long. You know how long we've waited. Then we married, and for what? To wait again? Has there ever been an erection in this house? What gives, my husband?"

"I'd tell you if I knew. Maybe I wouldn't act a thousand if you didn't act sixteen."

"I do it to turn you on, for godsake!" She grew thoughtful. "Maybe it's the games," she said as she rewrapped herself in her silk robe. "If we tried not to play at these sexual encounters according to the Bible, maybe it would be better."

"Maybe," I said. "But fundamentally I think the games are great. I love the games, and I love you, Shulamit."

"Then why are you acting like an old fart, a real King David, nearly a dead man? I do not want to be married all my life to a dead man. Maybe toward the end, okay. But not at the beginning, Jonah. Please!"

And now, dear congregants, your outstanding patience, along with your only human curiosity, are finally rewarded with secrets about to be revealed in generally unadorned dialogue and narrative, without the slightest homiletical obfuscation: "I am a virgin!" she said to me for the millionth time. "A Jewish virgin. I am perhaps the last twenty-five-year-old Jewish virgin in the United States! I have been dreaming all my life of my marriage to you, Jonah, and of these days and nights together. I have been dreaming of the dresses and the nightgowns and the slippers and the peignoirs I would wear. So, all right, you buy me cheap pornographic under-wear, I can handle that. But I am pent up! I am saved up, Jonah. I am champing at the bit, my husband. Let's go, let's go! Day and night. In all the corners of this apartment. In all positions and varia-tions. According to all the positions of the *Kama Sutra* and the laws of Moses or in violation. In praise of God, of course. Take me, Jonah. I can hardly be held down and you know it. I am yours. Spin me like a dreidel. Knead me like a latke. Kiss me like you used to kiss the fringes of your tallis when I first prayed with you."—How long ago was that? My God, how long ago—"When I watched you do that, I said to myself, I want those lips on my lips, I can imagine those fingers touching my body. It's not as if I don't have the will, it's not as if I haven't tried!"

"Oh, you've tried," I said.

"Then do something, before I explode!"

Thus Brandy said to me months after our marriage; the preoccupation about my erectile dysfunction had set in, dear friends, growing worse and worse with each passing day, like the plagues in Egypt.

I began to busy myself with the many household chores that Brandy increasingly left undone, I imagined, in her frustration with me. I cooked, I kept the porcelain surfaces in the bathroom gleaming; I also built a rickety set of bookshelves. In general I avoided her eyes, especially during the tense evenings at home.

Brandy said she thought a different kind of bed, a water bed perhaps, might make a difference. Since neither of us had yet landed a full-time job and we had been living mostly off the wedding loot, which was now running low, I decided to build the bed myself. Wood wasn't terribly expensive, and water was free. A Jonah, I have always loved swimming in it and drinking it, so why not sleep upon it as well?

"Tell me what you're supposed to do if you make a bed," Brandy said to me one night as she slipped open her white silk robe once again all the way down to the omphalos.

I felt my heart pump a little faster and my stomach and bowels felt weak with an anxiety whose depths I had never known. I suppose it had always been intermingled with my attraction to Wild Thing, but, like some new germ I'd discovered, it had never been separated out until now.

"Well?" She undid the belt of her robe and slowly let it open. "What do you do?"

"If you make a bed," I said with feigned nonchalance, "you're supposed to . . . sand it."

"And what else?"

"Wax it."

She dropped the robe slowly all the way to the floor, revealing a very long branch of grapes that she had somehow hooked onto a green sash at her waist. "Is that all?" The grapes dropped in a descending branch from her belly button down toward her crotch, and spread out in and over her pubic hair.

"Paint it."

"What else?"

"Are they with seeds or without, Brandy?"

She paused, as nonplussed by my response, I believe, as I was by the sight before me, by turns paradisiac and pornographic. Then Brandy picked up the robe, pulled it around herself, and cried, "When you make a bed, you lie in it, Jonah!" Walking quickly down the hall and stopping for a second to perform an awkward gesture—I imagined, to hitch up the grapes and pop one in her mouth—she shouted, "For godsake, when you make a bed, you lie in it. With your wife!"

"I don't even like grapes!" I screamed after her. "You should know by now I don't like them!"

Shortly after this incident, I began to build our new bed in earnest. I worked very slowly and deliberately. First I researched a model by going through drawings in the how-to section of the bookstore. Then I drafted my variation with pencil, compass, and T square. This phase of the enterprise took two weeks.

I brought the wood home slowly, a few boards at a time, and stored them conspicuously in the long hall of our apartment. At the far end of the hall, in our bedroom, Wild Thing played rock music while I measured, sawed, planed, and drilled. Soon there was a sawhorse and cut pieces of wood all over the place, so that the apartment began to look more like a construction site than a love nest. One night when my drilling blew a fuse and knocked out the music during one Lovin' Spoonful song she particularly liked, Brandy stormed in and screamed, "This had better be good, Grief!"

"It will be," I assured her.

"But why can't you follow a plan instead of inventing your own? Won't that make it go faster? Aren't you tired of sleeping on the floor?"

"I don't like plans," I replied.

"Noah had one when he built the ark. Solomon had one when he built the temple! Even that idiot Gordon Liddy had a plan when he broke into the Watergate. Even a bad plan is better than no plan. Jonah, what's with you?"

"It doesn't need a plan because it's going to be a one-of-a-kind work of art," I told her—feebly, I know, but not without a nugget of truth—"worthy of you."

For weeks I continued to saw and drill every day, stopping only for the broadcast of the Watergate hearings, which I began to view as both my reward and my entertainment. On the night I finished the routing above my medley of designs—Stars of David, Lions of Judah, alligator skin cowboy boots, menorahs, covered wagons, wheatfields of Kansas, and, in the corner, on a far smaller scale, my signature item, Jonah and his fish—Brandy Lee was out at the movies for the first time without me. Soon she regularly began to spend a night or two a week out of the apartment. Movies, a play with her friends Ada or Lea, a visit to cousins in Washington Heights. There was also a series of lectures up at the Seminary given by one of its first female professors, on whether women were in attendance or were not when God revealed himself at Sinai. She began to talk about returning to school. I understood and I didn't object. Then one night she announced she was looking for full-time work.

During this period Big Lou, Arthur, Ronnie, and I tried to stay in touch. We met once every two or three weeks to play poker, to study a little together, and to exchange tips about pulpit openings. I did most of the arranging and calling. I realized it was a little like Junior Cong revisited, but it was oddly very important for me, so the calling was no burden at all. I also happily offered our apartment as the regular gathering place, usually on a night Brandy was out. I was not fully aware of it—I don't believe I was fully aware of anything then!—but something even more significant than my marriage was also gradually crumbling; I desperately needed the Questions near me, but they too had begun to grow very busy and were slipping away.

Of all of us, still only Ronnie had gotten a real pulpit—in an old community of Jewish chicken farmers in southern New Jersey. He seemed much less anxious, even close to being happy. Why? He was in love, quite literally, with one of the farmers' daughters, a big-boned (so I inferred from the snapshot he proudly carried in his wallet) and fair-haired woman named Dahlia. He barraged me with all kinds of questions about being a married man. Ronnie confessed that he'd always been attracted to big women, and Dahlia with her corn-fed skin and great strength—she chopped wood to heat the family house—was the creature of his dreams. I was, Ronnie said, his hero and mentor in the marriage department and he urged me to tell him everything. All the secrets to having a terrific, red-hot marriage, just like mine, was how he put it.

I couldn't bear to disappoint him with the truth of my situation. The best dissimulation I could come up with was to offer him some generalized advice, hoping not to reveal that it was as empty-headed, clichéd, and unempirical as Polonius's palaver to Laertes: "Go very slow," I told Ronnie. "Marriage is a serious institution. And it's no bowl of cherries either," I said quite unintentionally, and then tacked on what seemed like a chuckle required by our young masculinity.

Our game had, thankfully, begun. "Seven card stud or draw?" I asked eagerly.

There was no reason at all to think Ronnie's experience would be mine, and I saw no reason to spoil his rising optimism with detailed reports from my conjugal jungle. I knew I might divulge the whole mess if I got started, so I continued to be tight-lipped, aphoristic, cool. But who was I really fooling? At the end of a long night of cards, at about two in the morning, he asked me to be his best man if he got married. I answered with groggy sarcasm that it depended on whether the Yankees or Mets were playing on the day of the joyous event. If not, I would be there.

A line of puzzlement moved along his face, truly goateed now with his first rabbinical beard, but looking somehow more Foo Manchu-ish than Jewish. "You're being very peculiar."

"Just the same old me," I said. "Of course I'll be there. Just don't rush into things is all I'm saying."

"Did you?"

"Rush is not the operative word for me," I believe I answered. "Stumbled. I have stumbled a little, but not to worry."

Not to worry! The other Questions reached out to me, in their own way, but my embarrassment and growing sense of failure, dear congregants, gradually made me like a defective telephone with my friends, either mute or shrill, with little voice in between. I dreaded their asking about Brandy and me, but fortunately soon there was much else to talk about—on their part. They seemed gradually, no, dramatically, in the space of months, so much more mature than I. Out here in "the real world," away from the protected precinct of the Seminary, where I guess it is fair to say that, academics notwithstanding, I had excelled as a personality, now my closest friends had all emerged into a bright, scintillating new light in which I saw their strengths as my weaknesses, their eager pursuit of their careers as my listless meandering. Their Jewish stars were now beginning to rise, while I remained barely stationary and had even begun to falter and fall. Compared to them, what had I become but a kind of smooth-talking married graduate student, halfheartedly looking for work but still thinking and acting as if life were another course I was enrolled in?

I was confused, my conjugal condition was one of perpetual anxiety, lethargy and dread were mounting like rising flood waters. In the evenings, at home with Brandy, I began to suffer from very time-consuming bowel movements that I disingenuously blamed on excessive consumption at the deli. Hiding from my own wife's penetrating eyes, I grew angry and jealous, and the more I craved the Questions' company the less I felt I could show my need for it.

My fellow congregants! At the half-year point out of rabbinical school, of all the Four Questions, your rabbi was definitely the most stuck. Arthur decided the rabbinical route he originally had contemplated was, after all, not for him. Then he promptly landed two college jobs—teaching Kabalistic and Hasidic literature and thought. One was at City University, one at the Jesuit seminary. Evenings he began studying Hinduism and working at an occult bookstore downtown. He was considering opening one of his own that carried books on spirituality of all faiths and persuasions. It was a great idea but he had no capital and he certainly couldn't raise it from the likes of us. His Barnard girlfriend, the one who had spoken in tongues, went back home to Georgia to enter her father's church. Arthur, not one to be lonely too long, had already begun to date a Japanese woman who taught at a Karate academy by day and at night studied computers.

Big Lou announced one evening over a run of two straights, a flush, and four of a kind that he was enrolled in a psychoanalytic institute in New Jersey, studying there to become a therapist. In the meantime he was paying tuition and supporting himself by teaching Hebrew school at seven different temples in three states. Count them! There were Temple Beth Sholom and Congregation B'nai Sholom in New York, and Temple Beth David and Beth Ami in southern Connecticut. Anshe Chesed and Anshe Or were in New Jersey, and only forty-five miles apart. For a change of pace he spent the sabbath as a part-time chaplain, driving his rusted-out Honda to visit Jewish convicts in penitentiaries in the Hudson River Valley. Except for the prisons, where he had two Orthodox, one Conservative, and three Reform Jews doing time, on any given day Lou might not actually know which school he was at, or which lesson he was teaching.

But it was all right; one lesson merged into another, and the trunk of Lou's car soon could barely be slammed shut, overflowing as it was with boxes crammed with hundreds of ditto sheets— Hebrew crossword puzzles, Bible stories, and exercises, his favorite being a blank decalogue where the kids got to write their own Ten Commandments. Lou was saving the very best responses—one little boy had written quite creatively, Lou thought, "Thou shalt not kill your mother and your father"—intending to call the child's parents and suggest immediate long-term family therapy, once he got his credential.

Often Lou confused the names of the temples, the various Michaels, Rachels, Davids, and Sarahs, and his coworkers' names as well. No matter. His whirlwind style, his eclecticism, and his impro- visational verve made Lou a cynosure to which kids, teachers, and temple educational directors— all absolutely desperate for some Jewish pizzazz—were thoroughly attracted. He also liked to be paid in cash. He thought of himself as a kind of rabbi-on-call—and was he not?—an entire mobile one-man Jewish school system in a Honda. Although he often got lost on the homogeneously landscaped suburban roads, on which his seven or eight temples were planted, and showed up late to class, his shirt dangling over his belt, breathless and clinging to his briefcase that often unlatched during the sprint across the parking lot, Big Lou somehow carried it all off.

How I loved his stories! How I needed his life! And so, one day, inspired—and shamed—by Big

Lou's enterprise, I screwed my rabbinical courage to the sticking place, and, taking a compass, drew a circle on a road map with a radius of one hundred miles from the Seminary in all directions. Within this area I resolved to get interviews for all vacant pulpit and educational positions.

However, each of the calls I made somehow chipped away a piece of my courage. During the half dozen interviews I was able to secure, I was consistently nervous and self-conscious. I sensed my interlocutors astonishingly bored within minutes of my opening my mouth, which was not a good sign as most of the congregations sought a charismatic leader—so read the job descriptions—able to draw new members into the temple family. They only perked up when, and if, I mentioned Brandy Lee and the distinguished Snyder family name.

I persisted, but soon began to have disturbing and debilitating dreams featuring members of all the search committees with whom I had interviewed. Here were the associate, assistant, senior, visiting, and emeritus rabbis, the junior and assistant cantors, the successful businessmen, the presidents, vice-presidents, and treasurers, the lay leaders and fundraisers, the Hebrew school administrators and temple executive directors, the secretaries and the gift-shop managers, even the deferential, black, yarmulke-wearing janitors, whose presence at all the temples of my life, as far back as my halcyon Junior Cong days, has always both reassured and disturbed me—I imagined all these figures in a kind of Talmud Torah variation of a danse macabre, passing my resumé from hand to quivering hand. And there in a huge, bold, seraphic typeface is what each of them reads aloud, in turn: Jonah Grief, Columbia, B.A., 1967; Jewish Theological Seminary, ordained, and married, 1972; Impotent, 1973.

How slowly days of impotence pass, dear friends! It was now eight months into the marriage and your Jonah felt miserable and ashamed. And yet he was doing precious little, either as husband or rabbi. I was stuck in the belly of the great fish, in the pit of a marriage I should never have entered, swallowed up, feeding upon the unsatisfying krill of confusion and self-pity. Until then my life had always seemed infused with purpose, movement, a sense of progress, and even a kind of ascension, all of which I had left fundamentally unquestioned, but I now found myself suddenly and horribly stripped down and bereft. I was living off our marriage savings, with nothing to proclaim, to truly believe, or even to do. Brandy took trips home to Kansas, she was a substitute teacher, but most of all she seemed to be waiting for me to make my moves. Yet all I had become was the mad and tedious maker of a water bed frame!

I now began to watch the Watergate hearings unfold with a growing fascination. By day and often by night in the increasingly lonely apartment—even the thick, exciting smells of her cosmetics had begun to evaporate—I watched the hearings commented upon, obsessively reviewed, and then rebroadcast.

There was something deeply personal for me and oddly reassuring in all this public probing. While I wanted to identify with the investigative heroes, with Sam Dash and Sam Ervin and the others, I knew I could not. Somehow it was the culprits with whom I felt closest, particularly with the Kafkaesque Nixon, a man so unreliable and troubled that he seemed to be living a secret impenetrable even to himself. Was that the reason he—I—felt so hurt, so aghast at being pursued and maybe found out? I too had embarrassing and terrible secrets, but I seemed to need if not a prosecution then at least a public to tell them to, before whom I could explain, justify, and analyze. Simply telling the truth, without the adornments of attention and hoopla, would be insufficient.

As my unhappiness grew, I actually began to seek solace in prayer, the only way I knew how at the time. During the lunch recesses and other breaks in the hearings, for the first time in months I thumbed through siddur and Bible. I went off to the corner of the room, as I remembered my chayder teacher had done, and kicked clear a spot amid piles of my jeans and T-shirts, Brandy's underwear, her bobbe-knitted angora sweaters, and all our disconsolate, holey, unmatched socks littering the bedroom floor. There, surrounded by our college books, many still crated, unread, and unloved, I rocked back and forth in traditional Jewish prayer desperately trying to find kavanah, meaning and transport to a realm of relief.

I was very primitive, my friends, and thought of God at such times as a kind of heavenly aspirin. I prayed with fervor, but so many of the words now sounded odd and even alien, as if they were only sound, their doxological supplications and repeated transcendental nudging—all that annoying Adonai-ing—were as suspect to my own ears, listening in judgment of my lips, as the canned and rehearsed testimony of Chapin, Liddy, Ehrlichman, and Haldeman. I could not believe they would be efficacious.

Mercy began to arrive one beautiful night in July, 1973, I believe, when the doorbell rang during the replay of the testimony of Attorney General John Mitchell. As usual, Brandy was out, and Lou was coming over to give me some job information about a place called the United Hebrew Alliance of Kleinkill; it was the eighth or perhaps ninth synagogue that wanted to hire him as occasional rabbi. He was drawing the line, however; he'd go mad if he took on another job, and so the position was mine, he had said, if I wanted it. But Lou, to whom I had confided, in part, my ludicrous and agonizing sexual state, had, as it turned out, another purpose as well.

Big Lou entered, and along with him, a head taller, Ada Karp, Brandy's Barnard roommate, whom I had not seen in many months. She had decided against medical school and had gotten a good job instead at the ichthyology department of the Museum of Natural History.

"Notice my eyes," she said after a warm and friendly kiss. "I find that since I've begun working with fish, who sleep with their eyes open, I blink less and less."

"Ada's also into some very smooth hash," Lou added.

It did not escape me, as it does not you, that I was a Jonah and she an expert in fish.

Straight away we moved the sawhorses that partially barricaded the entrance hall, then my oversupply of two-by-fours, my bags of nails and screws, and my circular saw on its stand. We stepped over the tumulus of wood dust and shavings that for some reason I was lovingly keeping, and sat down on the floor. I lit Ada's hash pipe with my best wood-burning auger.

Thanks to the midwifery of Ada's smooth stuff from Morocco, I more or less fell apart before them. Maybe I was just so pent up, so poised for confession, that I would have talked as freely and openly had the electric company meter-reader been at the door. But something about Ada's presence seemed to suggest that nothing would shock or bother her. And when she tossed her curly head back and yawned a big gaping yawn, showing a healthy red palate and the roof of her mouth, it all reminded me in miniature of what I had been reading: Jonah and what he must have beheld as he slid down his fish's throat. Had she really said she was an ichthyologist? When Ada's lively face finally settled into a smile of weary contentment, I felt the lump develop, slow, pleasing, and reassuring—my first sexual stirring in what seemed like a millennium.

"United Hebrew Alliance of Kleinkill is about a hundred twenty miles up the Hudson." Lou interrupted my reverie and, through a plume of smoke, he continued, "It has perhaps fourteen active members left, and not a one under age sixty-five." He was reading from one of the note cards he habitually carried in his back pocket to remind him of where he was and whom he was teaching. "The last bar mitzvah held was, I believe, shortly before FDR took office for his first term. It's the only community shul exempt from the UJA-Federation campaign because it's not worth the trouble to raise funds there." Big Lou sighed, paused. "A retired dentist, named Nathan Demmick, runs the whole show: president of the congregation, Torah reader, buys the kiddush wine, and sweeps up afterward himself. A regular one-man band." Lou put his nose down closer to his index card to decipher his own scrawl. "'They run from me twice,' he's quoted as saying. 'First because I'm a dentist and they think I'll hurt them. And, second, because they think I'm after their money. A family sees me coming just to wish them good shabbos and they deliberately cross the street. It's no wonder we don't raise much. It's a little disheartening. Fortunately I am an optimist.' So much for President Demmick," Lou went on. "The building's also falling down, but there's at least a decent view of orchards and the river and a nice large green lawn for the youth groups to play ball; unfortunately, there are no youth groups. United Hebrew Alliance of Kleinkill, known as UHAK, is almost certainly on its last legs as a Jewish institution. Rabbi Jonah Grief, this shul was made in heaven just for an impotent . . . for you!"

"Done?"

"Yes," he said, "and forgive me if I've embarrassed you in front of Ada. If I'm crass," he giggled, "blame the grass. But she's heard."

"You told her?"

"If your pecker's in trouble, that's my concern as much as your pulpit."

"Because the mind and body are connected," Ada said. She inhaled deeply and added, "At least in fish."

I could have died. Maybe, dear congregants, I did die then. There are so many little dyings in life, wrote a great Zen poet of the sixties whose name will never come to me, it's impossible to know which is truly Death. "You have definitely told her, Lou?"

"Most definitely," he answered, between deep draws on the hash pipe.

"Don't be old-fashioned," Ada said, with a decidedly old-fashioned smile of reassurance. "Think of me not as Brandy's former roommate, but as a scientist.

"Look," she said sweetly, "we all have trouble once in a while. Anyway, Brandy's virginity was universal knowledge at Barnard, and, I suppose, beyond."

"True," Lou mumbled. "Truer than true."

"But did *you* know," Ada said to me, with that smile again, "when you began to date?"

"I may not have done well in school but I'm not a total idiot. Of course I knew," I cried. "I just didn't realize . . . the degree to which she was a virgin."

"Meaning what, rabbi?" said Ada.

"Meaning how much she focused on it. How important it is to her. How important ending it is, I mean. To say she now expects a lot is to state the obvious of the obvious. Of course, I can't blame her. In principle. That's why she married me."

"You're just a man," Ada answered. "A rabbi-type man, to be sure, and you only have what you have!" Which was when I realized my erection was quite visible. I quickly crossed my legs to settle it in. "At least we have determined that there is no phys- iological problem with the male of the couple."

I believe I bowed slightly toward Ada, with a gratitude she could not imagine.

"Now let me try to understand this impotence," she went on. "Is it that you're afraid of Brandy? She is a daunting personality."

"I wouldn't say fear's the issue."

"If not fear," Lou mumbled through half-closed eyes and mouth. "Then what's the problem?"

"It's not as if nothing has happened," I protested. "Everything has happened."

"And yet she's still a virgin?" Lou stammered.

How I wanted to confess absolutely everything then! Yet, as you well know, confession can be just another form of subterfuge. And was your rabbi not concealing the main lie, and wondering at the same time if Ada or Lou had already guessed it?

After a long silence, Ada said, "I really encouraged her, Rabbi Grief. I admired her high standards, but since I had slept with more boys by then than I cared to remember, I thought it would be a good change of pace for both of us if I abstained for a while, and she picked up the ball, so to speak. A kind of conservation of screwing in the universe. I remember having that discussion with Brandy," she went on, "and I urged her without reservation to become involved, to enjoy it."

"It?"

"You, rabbi."

"I'm indebted to you, I guess."

"You still don't know what you want to do, do you, buddy?" Lou interjected. "Perhaps a little pastoral counseling is in order?" He inhaled deeply, he giggled, then he said, dropping into a low mock-psychoanalytic octave, "Perhaps you should see your rabbi."

"Please pass the pipe, Rabbi Grief," Ada said suddenly, "and tell me as Brandy Lee's ex-roommate who advised her to sleep with you, why is she still a virgin? I demand an immediate answer."

I shrugged and sighed and yearned for Ada to throw her arms around my neck, cover my face with soft kisses, and whisper things ichthyological in my ears. I felt suddenly adulterous in my thoughts, but at least adulterously alive.

Before I could answer, or rather, marshal my dissembling defenses once again, Lou said, "He's not sleeping with her because he doesn't want to consummate the marriage. It's that simple. Isn't that right, Jonah? Like his glass-breaking trick at the wedding. I know this character." Big Lou went on with hashish-augmented clarity: "I know all his moves. He's like the young king with his queen. When the servants come in the morning to check if there's blood on the sheets and if the marriage is therefore legal and the realms are joined and the future offspring legitimate, when that happens, Grief wants not a spot to be found."

"But why?" Ada asked. "Are you afraid she's going to swallow it up?"

"I like your directness," I told Ada.

"I apologize," she answered, "but a man who is aggressively, solidly impotent for a year has to have a reason. Because Lou has told me of your affinity for Jonah, I thought fear of being overwhelmed and swallowed—a common enough problem among males of the species—might be a real candidate for the answer. But you are obviously not a garden variety case. So, if I'm wrong, I'm wrong, and it's on to the next bowl of hash. Another hypothesis? Rabbi?"

I appreciated Ada's effort—Lou was by now quite nearly asleep—and I struggled to find accurate words to describe what it was that had occurred between Brandy and me. "It's more like a feeling I get that she considers my penis something separate from me. Does that make sense? With a life and function and predilection of its own, apart from me, from the rest of me. I often catch her looking at me below the waist, contemplating my crotch."

"A lot of men would consider you a lucky guy."

"I know it sounds too good to be true. And I know how great we look on paper, but somehow it stops there. It's hard to explain; it's as if she's chosen me to mate with in order to end her virginity. It's as if I'm an instrument."

"And what's wrong with that?" Ada said. "Someone's got to do it."

"Yes," I protested, "but where's the meeting of minds between us? Am I being too romantic? Where are our souls and minds coming together, being expressed through our bodies?"

With her elbow, Ada nudged Lou in the ribs. One of his eyes was now partially opened, reminding me of a pirate's. But he was still out. "Grief, honestly, what kind of meeting of minds do you expect? She's so much smarter than you—than any of us."

"True enough. But I'm not talking about Talmud or Spinoza. I'm talking about things like openness, easy, casual conversation about everything under the sun. Like this! How about friendship!"

"Let's just get to the mechanics of the intercourse part," Lou mumbled to Ada in his half-sleep, "just to make sure he's checked out."

"I don't think we can do that tonight," Ada said, tiredly and wisely. "I'm beat."

With that implication of future get-togethers like this one, I was inspired to go on, and on. "We have so much ill feeling on the way to bed, by the time we get there we're already quarreling and it's hopeless. I try and she tries, Lord knows, but there's something about her biology and mine that's like oil and water. No mixing, and barely any touching, these days." Ada was nodding her head, Lou was snoring. "Maybe," I said, "we've had enough for one night?"

"Mmm."

"What I'm trying to get at," I went on, feeling safer now, "is that the very thought of sleeping with Brandy is like not sleeping with a single human being at all, a young beautiful woman, but rather with this vast suppressed urge. It's like sleeping with the whole Labor Zionist movement, the entire lusty yearning Middle East, or is it the Middle West? With Lilith and the Shechinah, the female side of the deity, the whole ball game! I had absolutely no idea whatsoever what I was getting into. Have I told you about the grapes and the garter belts?"

"Mmm," came the answer. I believe it was from Ada.

"And the requests for spankings?"

"Mmm."

"Does anyone understand this? Does the fantasy life take a weird turn when it is wrapped up too long and too tightly in the robes of faith? Well, isn't it the very opposite of what you would think might occur when two people of our backgrounds approach each other on the conjugal bed?"

"Mmmmmm."

"And there's one thing more I've failed to mention that might have some bearing on this problem." I waited for a sign of consciousness from Ada or Lou. When I saw that they were both asleep I said it: "I'm also a virgin."

So there! The secret was out, my congregants! I had said it anyway, within easy earshot of my friends who were probably too stoned to hear. If you think the less of me for it, for my shame and concealment at the time, and indeed throughout my Seminary life, I don't blame you. Not at all. The Lothario of the Seminary, the Hebrew Don Juan had been a fraud.

But wasn't this marriage my comeuppance? With all the other scholars to choose from, with Big Lou, who was so good-looking, and so many others, why had Brandy Lee Snyder chosen me?

Our tradition requires an explanation, a commentary.

Incidentally, if there is a statement made, such as the confession of my own virginity and the hearers were asleep, can it be said that confession occurred? Accordingly, if there is revelation, and no people at Sinai or elsewhere to hear and record it, did it occur?

My sleepy ones! The incident just related took place around eleven o'clock in the spring of the Jewish year 5,734, that is, 1973. We have left Big Lou and Ada dozing. I myself had fallen briefly asleep, but then woke up and roused my friends from their haze. Lou left me the papers from the United Hebrew Alliance of Kleinkill, and I thanked him for that, although I somehow knew I would not pursue it. Ada gave me a kiss far more demure than the one she had offered on arriving, as if what she had heard during the course of the evening had somehow set her, not surprisingly, on her guard.

"Thank you," I remember her saying, "for one of the least boring evenings I've spent in a long time."

I was very grateful to both of them. Shortly before midnight, leaning on each other, my friends departed.

About an hour later I was still awake and turning fitfully in my sleeping bag amid the two-by-fours beside the not-quite-finished water bed frame when I heard Brandy's steps in the hall.

Where had she been? It had gotten so bad between us, I didn't even know. But even at this hour, her perfume was still strong. I closed my eyes as she stepped over me and paused, her long legs straddling me like a pyramid, like a miniskirted Deborah or Jael or Judith over her fallen foe, an enemy of Israel.

"Are you awake, Jonah?" she asked. "If you are, don't fake that you're not."

Oddly, I felt, for the first time in months, real tenderness toward Brandy. Some bitterness had lifted and made room within me to see and feel how lovely her body truly was. I was suddenly full of such compassion for our mutual innocence and for the mess that we had somehow thrust on each other, that I thought, yes, maybe we can work it out, maybe I should again try making love with her. Nevertheless, I just lay there, and the all-too-familiar web of sexual paralysis began to wrap around me from within.

In retrospect, perhaps this was the night, and this the interval of perhaps fifteen minutes—between the time she entered the apartment and the time she finished brushing her teeth and readying for sleep—that the marriage shifted on its fragile fulcrum and failure became inevitable. As the great monk Narihiri has written, "I have always known that at last I would take this road, but yesterday I did not know that it would be today."

I lay there listening to the water sounds she made and then to her footsteps out of the bathroom, back down the hall, up to and beside me, where she paused, thinking thoughts I will never know. Then she walked over to the couch, which she had been sleeping on for the past weeks. I realized then this was perhaps a last attempt to bridge the chasm, to get closer to me in my sleeping bag, where I lay some six feet away, and within view. "Lila tov," she said in a sad, lilting Hebrew. "Good night." Then she began singing verses of a Jewish camp song we used to sing at lights-out. I'm certain she arced the words to me: "Lila tov, shemesh dom hacochavim notz-zim, bamarom, shalom . . . shalom—Good night, the sun is still, the stars are twinkling, in the vault of heaven, good night . . . good night."

GIMMEL

THE LONG OVERDUE CONFESSION of my virginity, rehearsed before my dozing friends, was now at long last ready to bring before my wife. I refer to the night of August 18, 5,734 Jewish years since the original sex scenes took place behind the apple tree in the humid Garden of Eden.

Our watery garden—Brandy and I were finally on the new water bed—was holding up quite nicely. The nearby shelves were piled high with her sweaters, the corners overflowing with her boots, and socks, and my stuff everywhere, too. The set of Talmud, barely opened by either of us since leaving school, stood forlornly on a line of green Dellwood milk crates at the foot of the bed. We had just finished watching the rebroadcast of testimony by James McCord, Bud Krogh, John Dean, and a few other Watergate crooks, and we were drifting off to sleep. As usual, no sex.

Earlier in the evening Brandy was reading the paper, bringing to the daily headlines the same intent concentration she brought to everything. I was flipping through the dial to watch the hearings. As usual, we were ignoring each other. Sum total of

Brandy's clothing was a bra with a pink rose at the cleavage as from a birthday cake. Her ass was bare and white and your rabbi was studying it like a page of hypnotic text, the follicles and freckles like a scribe's pintlach, the marks and vowels on the vellum. Your rabbi was in blue jeans, white T-shirt, and white sweat socks—a puerile outfit, to be sure. Brandy suddenly raised herself on her hands, unfastened her bra, pulled up her right haunch for balance, and turned down the TV volume.

"Talk to me," she said, curling up beside me naked as a snail slipped out of its shell. "Tell me what you're thinking. Then make love to me, Jonah. Or, conversely, make love to me first and we'll discuss the problem later. In any case, let us be optimists, let us do it! Let us try again."

"'Tis a consummation," I murmured, "devoutly to be wished."

"Jonah," she said, mockingly. "Honored and revered husband! You're being a total jerk!"

"I couldn't agree more."

"What is wrong, Jonah?"

"What good does it do to go over it again?"

"So why don't you pull the sheet up over your head right now the way you always end up doing!"

"Okay," I said, "I will."

We fell silent and eased away from each other to watch Maureen Dean, cool, blonde, imperturbable behind her husband as the President's counsel lied or told the truth or, like me, floundered between the two, not knowing what the truth was.

"Do you know why we watch this, Jonah? Day and night?" she began. "We watch this not only because Watergate has become a substitute for sex between us, but because it would take a five-million-dollar national inquiry for me to understand what your problem is. I mean, look at me! I'm naked! I'm beautiful, if I do say so myself, which I will, since you never say it! It is no longer funny, Jonah, that you live for Watergate and hide under a white sheet all by yourself as if you were a piece of covered furniture in a house where someone has died. Gott in Himmel," she cried, the phrase and the pain of her voice also the pain of her bobbes of the Midwest and of Jewish wives over thousands of years, the wives of the Gemara and Mishna era complaining about their withdrawn, over-studious husbands, and the Roman and Greek ones, the Yemenite and Ethiopian Jewish wives, the Jewish wives of Copenhagen and of Tierra del Fuego, the Jewish wives before their puny little husbands, women of iron, the Deborahs and Judiths and Jaels before the timid and mushy men of Judah.

"We've talked and talked," I said. "It doesn't seem to help."

"Darling," she said, rappeling up and onto my prone form just as Senator Ervin gaveled the proceedings to order and started his mellifluous cross-examination. "Darling, oh, darling," she cried. Her mouth was all over me, wet and generous, but, God help me, I was irritated because I couldn't see the Senator over Brandy's wild hair. Voluptuously, she undressed me. "We are two naked people," she cried breathlessly, "one male, one female. Let us become one flesh."

"Please, Brandy."

"Spank me, Jonah. Will that help?"

"Not at all. It's you who likes that."

"Fruit tonight? Grapes?"

"I'm sick of fruit."

"You act as if something terrible is wrong with me."

"There is something terrible going on here, but please don't take it personally."

"You always say that. How can a person—and I am a person—not take everything personally, especially your rejection of my naked flesh!"

"I am not rejecting you," I said.

"No. Only the idea of me, the concept of me! My spirit, too!" At which we both looked down at Old King David, who just dangled there limp as always like a willow branch by the windless waters of Babylon. Nothing stirred. It was then I realized I had to be out with it.

"I've got a confession to make."

"Yes?"

Brandy sat up and uncharacteristically covered her nakedness. I put the bottom sheet over her exposed feet.

"I've been a faker, a big one, and I'm sorry. I'm sorry for all the pain I've caused you. It wasn't intentional, but I take responsibility completely, for whatever that's worth. There, that's it, Brandy. All there is to it."

"To what?"

"I didn't say it?"

"Jonah, you've been watching the hearings too much."

"I don't know how to put this. I think fundamentally it has nothing to do with our problem, but here goes: I'm a virgin. Just like you."

I watched her eyes. She waited, and I wondered what she was thinking. She didn't laugh and no line of scorn revealed itself on her face, for which I was grateful; yet it was just as disconcerting that her eyes told me nothing. I didn't feel any particular relief. I felt strangely distant, my secret having come out, and I could have stayed there for minutes, for hours, a whole life past and one yet to come, suspended in that moment.

I felt tender toward Brandy and reached out to touch her soft face, but she would not let my gesture run its course. She headed off my hand with her own, squeezed it hard, and then lowered her face into my palm, kissing it. I was very moved. Quietly, but with ardor, she began to lick and then swallow a finger. Two, then three fingers in her mouth. Then she lapped at the crevices in between.

I tried to give myself up to the sensations, and to Brandy. "My God," she murmured, looking up at me, "two virgins! And it's my time, too. Who knows what we'll produce!"

I pulled my hand back. I heard her draw in her breath. I think there were tears welling in her eyes.

"I don't understand you, Jonah. Virgin or no virgin, I know you know *how* to do it," she said. "Eventually you'll get an erection. An erection is not a work of art. It is not nuclear physics. It is not Talmud. It is natural. You don't work at it. You let it develop. Shall I help you, my virgin, my rabbi?"

"I don't think so," I said. "Not tonight."

"Then when?"

How to put this? I said to her, "This is an important piece of news for you and you hardly take it in before you're all over me. Can't we talk first? Why must you always start licking me? Am I a pear or plum you've got to have your mouth around! Aren't you interested in why I've kept this from you all this time?"

"We've been talking for a year, Jonah. Don't think I didn't have my suspicions."

"Well, I am a virgin," I repeated, with an odd pride that surprised me. "All my carrying on at the Seminary was just a lot of bluster. I had to be good at something, so I chose my role, and even at that I faked it. You're married not only to a lousy rabbi but an impotent virgin as well. And a hypocrite. You deserve better."

"I deserve someone who does not sit and watch TV all day and night. I deserve someone who will try, who wants more in his life than Watergate and the Book of Jonah. If you're so full of revulsion for me, why did you marry me, someone who represents what you hate?"

"I never said I hated you."

"You don't have to say it. You don't have to say anything ever again!"

So I said, "The hearings are about to resume."

And she replied, slowly, "Fuck you. Fuck you, Jonah Grief."

"Never," I said. "If it matters to you so much, go fuck someone else. Fuck! Fuck! Fuck! How you like to say it! Fuck!" I screamed it out loud, my first sick and spontaneous mantra: "Fuck! Fuck!"

Oh my beloved congregants! How terribly good we can be at hurting one another! Before I could reach out to her again, she was up from the bed, wrapped in the sheet, and walking down the hall. In a minute or so I began to hear water filling the tub. I tortured myself with the thought that she again was going to wash away the shame of our failed attempt at consummation. It had happened so many times before. But this was different. Virginity was not the issue. That much I knew. Nor was it so terrible to be virgins, male and female. There were plenty more of us in the 1960s, in that bed-hopping era, who disguised our inexperience with borrowed bravura. For all I knew Lou was a virgin, as well, and Ronnie too. Maybe that was why Ronnie had been fishing around so much, and I unable to talk to him. Big deal! There was no shame attached to any of this, was there? I am human, and therefore nothing human is alien from me. Who said that? Was it Rabbi Akiba or Walt Whitman? The only real shame comes from the hurt of representing yourself falsely to the world—and to a future wife.

And perhaps what was worse, to yourself! If I was guilty, I was guilty of a kind of false personal advertising. I wished Brandy Lee Snyder, my wife, no more pain.

The more I had these thoughts, the better I began to feel. If she still wanted to consummate the marriage, okay! I had given her a choice. My proverbial cards were on the table.

I got up and stretched, turned the TV back on and, lo, when I looked away from the screen, there was action way down at the crossroads! I would go and tell Brandy that with my secret out, Old King David was now set free, at least for tonight.

In three or four testosterone-inspired steps I reached the bathroom door, but I found it uncharacteristically pulled shut and, apparently, latched. After a moment's hesitation, I knocked. Brandy did not answer. "Senator Ervin's going to be on next," I whispered. "Then Haldeman's making his statement. Brandy?" I heard her splashing. With the other ear I also picked up Walter Cronkite's voice, full of grave implications for the Republic. "Let's watch for an hour and then try again. Okay?"

There was more than no answer. There was a deep and watery quiet. Then the terrible thought rose up, a clichéd but nevertheless awful scene sketched itself out in my mind. Was it possible that Brandy, now with the admission of my own virginity, had suddenly become so desperate with sadness and hopelessness about our married life and what she would have to say to her family if we unraveled into divorce that she had been driven to take an extreme step in this locked room: to disrobe, to fill the tub with warm water, to enter the tub with razor blade in hand? And now the blade is fallen on the bathmat, and Brandy's wrists are slit, and the hot water is running red with her Orthodox Jewish blood?

So I did something, dear congregants, criminologists, and retired sex therapists, that may well have done us in for good, although at the time I thought a life was at stake: I took the letter opener and lifted the latch on the bathroom door.

I stepped in and saw her form behind the gray shower curtain. I parted it, and there she was. Not dead at all, but stretched luxuriously out in the lavender-scented bath water. There was indeed red in the tub: her cheery toenails protruding above the water line at the far end like colorful channel markers. Her face seemed to float upon the water as if by itself, eyes closed and profoundly relaxed and beautiful, but it made me think of the release of death as well. Then I saw the plastic penis and a round cake of soap languidly bobbing above her belly.

"Well what did you expect?" she said. "A smoking gun? I'm only human."

I lifted the object carefully out of the water like a prize fish. I believe I had always known of its existence, but with a denial I had become well practiced at, I imagined it had lived quietly and unused beneath Brandy's underwear in the top drawer of the dresser—reserved for yet untried contortions, entrances, and exits. I turned it around in a kind of awe. "It's awfully large," I said. "How does it feel?"

"I have precious little to compare it too, dear husband! Now go to your hearings and to your Senator Sam Ervin and leave my vibrator and me alone." Whereupon she quickly grabbed it back, and a wave of bath water spilled onto the floor.

It was not death, but pleasure and release that my wife was engaging in. I had not driven her to suicide, but to her own resources. And this understanding liberated me, made me experience a lightness I could not recall feeling before.

Then questions came raining down on me, questions I had never truly asked, like my own internal impeachment proceeding: My life had some greatness in it, did it not? Some possibility for true service, did it not? Isn't that why I had gone to the Seminary? Is that not why I had become a rabbi? Perhaps even married Brandy? And then another thought hit me with all the life-changing power of revelation: I hadn't really *gone* to the Seminary. And I hadn't really *chosen* Brandy either. I asked myself what the act of choosing might feel like, and I came up wanting. I hadn't chosen. Like a Jonah, I had been selected and sent!

Sent being the operative word of my existence. Sent! I repeated it aloud, another dumb mantra, and I wondered in my exegetical spasms how it might be related to *scent*. If the "c" had dropped out, and along with it all the intuition and self-knowledge *scent* implies, it left me only *sent*, an empty vessel of a verb. A passive verb implying that the power is elsewhere—in a powerful sender. Sent by others, by my family, my teachers, by Brandy. And now? Could I trust what was happening now?

These thoughts wrapped themselves about me, deeply disturbing yet also oddly regenerative. Was I not slow and confused precisely because something roiling and volcanic was amassing within? My life was not over, I was not consigned to being a c-minus Talmudist in a tortured marriage. While I was still not sure how to distinguish action from inaction, I knew something was beginning and the first step that I marked as truly my own was going to be the painful dissolution of my brief marriage.

The Watergate investigations went on that night until maybe one in the morning. That night, dear friends, for the first time, I was hit with a flash of insight into what pattern my life had taken—and would continue to take—unless I took action immediately. Yes, I wasn't going to be a pulpit rabbi like Ronnie. I had no patience for the daily round of petty kvetching that filled a rabbi's ear. Nor would I teach philosophy—not that I knew any, like Arthur—nor would I give it all up for the easily understood but illusory constructs of psychology like Big Lou. What was my calling? Hell, I didn't know specifics but clearly I was destined to be the truest Jew of all, the outsider, the gadfly, the troublemaker, the cryer-outer. Do I not talk and complain too much? And what of Jonah and Amos, Joel and Habbakuk? The prophet is characteristically a kvetch, a whiner, an insufferable one. No wonder they were either ignored or stoned.

Beloved congregants, I concluded that I was truly the fellow who has spent his whole life in an awkward and painful state, composed half of heresy and half of devotion, a man caught between flight and obedience. A Jonah indeed, I was growing minute by agonizing minute into my name.

As the senators and congressmen talked on into that night—and for many nights afterward, on into the impeachment hearings of 1974—I listened, desperately trying to make light of my situation but knowing self-deprecation too was a form of flight. One night, after the hearings concluded, a rerun of *What's My Line?* came on, and I imagined Jonah making an appearance as the secret guest, walking out in his blue-and-white kaftan to answer the questions of the blindfolded panelists: Do you, Mr. Amittai, deal in a product or services? Oh, services! Most definitely services.

When I realized I was destined, that is, being used, for this prophet's role, I found it initially exhilarating, and, as I have also mentioned, a frightening and not quite believable fate. There was something about it both arrogant and laughable, antimodern and deeply irrational. And yet it had all the urgency of true feeling.

Some weeks later, with sex still looming between us like an immense marquee without words, Brandy and I were sitting on our living room floor after we had finished a joyless meal of kosher moo goo gai pan and I said: "Isn't it best to end this before it gets worse? There are no kids, we haven't bought much, there's no property, we don't have to argue. Let's just separate."

Afterward, there followed weeks of crying, fighting, and pain, as when any bond is severed. At last Brandy gave me up, and we both gave one another up again and again, as these things happen. Then we began to argue about the sticks of our furniture. We had five director's chairs, which we divided, three for her, two for me. I didn't mind; I didn't expect more than one guest at a time and in fact wanted to see no one. Brandy didn't want the water bed, of course, or the shelves I had built for her, but she did prize the green leather sofa. It was where she had lain all those nights without me while I floated, alone, a Jonah, of course, on my water bed.

Even though I easily understood why she was attached to it, my congregants, I discovered I did not want to let Brandy have the sofa easily. Oh, no! As it was, we had agreed she would stay in the apartment and I would be the one to wander off across the city to find new lodgings. I anticipated that a grim doors-shut-in-the-face kind of fate awaited me. It made me feel cold and ungenerous. I had very little money and I thought I could at least sell the sofa and keep half the proceeds to pay a deposit on a new apartment—

and, in so doing, also get rid of the place she had lain. So I held out and made her argue and wonder for days.

Although I felt myself possessed of this new knowledge of being impelled along, as I have been struggling to describe, by a prophetic pattern, or antipattern, when it came down to practical business I was no smarter than before. Ronnie was by now living with Dahlia and would soon marry her; I knew I couldn't bear the humiliation their happiness would cause me; plus, they lived in New Jersey. I called up Arthur, only to find that he had accepted, after, all, a job at a suburban synagogue in Stamford, Illinois. Even if it did not work out, as he suspected, he could put away some capital to open his bookstore of the occult and the spiritual, which he had not yet been able to get off the ground. I asked him if I might take over his apartment. Unfortunately, it had already been leased.

Next I called Big Lou, and, as usual, he came through for me. He lived in only one room clogged with mimeographed sheets for Hebrew school exercises and boxes of new psychology books, but there would always be room for Jonah. I spilled my heart out to Lou, and he said I could have the run of the place and as many revelations as I wanted. I told him I would stay in the corner, like another box of stuff, and he would hardly notice.

Brandy and I barely spoke, except about the most essential matters—the keys, which she wanted back from me, and all the blank checks from our joint account; she intended to open one in her name only.

It took me four days to pack and arrange to borrow Lou's car. Finally, Brandy and I were standing on the sidewalk in front of the building. I had two shopping bags beside me, and Big Lou's Hebrew-school Honda stood across the street, filled with my suitcases and a box of power tools. Brandy seemed to me a woman I would like to meet—in ten or twenty years, when perhaps I might finally be grown up. She stood beside me fidgeting but glowing in her tight blue jeans, her boots, and tank top with a picture of Mt. Scopus. I felt a fool for leaving. The anxiety, tenderness, and tears I had been struggling to control for weeks now seemed about to overwhelm me. I wanted to hug or at least kiss her, but she gave me no opening. "Brandy," I finally said, "Jonah son of Amittai's wife could not have been half as beautiful as you."

She answered me: "What about the sofa?"

"I've been thinking about it."

"As I have. But it was bought with marriage gifts. It's as much yours as mine. We've played a lot of biblical games in our relationship, Jonah Grief. How about getting your saw and you begin to cut it in half like the baby in front of Solomon. We'll see who it bothers the most."

"I understand your anger," I said.

"Do more than understand it!" she screamed. "I'd like you to take it in, absorb it, and let it eat your heart out. Oh, Jonah! We could have been such a special couple."

"I'm sorry we screwed up," I said. And then a thousand "I'm sorrys" poured out of me like the litany of Al Chayts we recited earlier today, my congregants. Sorry for the sin of not listening enough and for being selfish. Sorry for being petty and self-involved. Sorry for being lazy. Sorry for watching too many hours of the Watergate hearings. Sorry for earning so little money. "I'm sorry," I concluded, "that we didn't screw enough. Didn't do it at all. I'm sorry it was all such a disappointment. I'm sorry you're still a virgin."

"Don't you worry," she answered. "I won't remain one much longer."

And thus, beloved congregants and meditators, that was how, many years ago, my marriage spewed me up onto dry land and I began my journey back here, to you and to this place, our synagogue by the runways, our little Nineveh-by-the-sea. Sometimes it is all so clear, so simple, a text without need for commentary. As Basho has written:

The old pond
A frog jumps in
Plop!

Within a month I found a place to live. It was a rooming house on the west side, where for twenty-five dollars a week I shared a floor with two single Cubans and one divorced salesman; one of the

Cubans was named Fredo de Leon, I never learned the name of the second, and the divorced man was Hal. I had a narrow living room with a sink on the wall, a sleeping alcove into which the water bed fit perfectly. There was a bath in the hall, and a kitchen whose fixtures had not been touched since the Depression.

The electricity was all right most days of the week. On summer evenings, however, with the air conditioners rattling away, the fuses tended to blow, plunging the entire building into darkness.

The owner, Mickey, a balding and reclusive Holocaust survivor who dealt in rare books, lived alone in the basement apartment. After paying my deposit and first month's rent, I saw Mickey only a few times a year for all the time I lived in his building. At least once a year, and usually on Yom Kippur, however, he labored up the dusty steps. With his breath wheezing, he stood and knocked on the door of my room. When I answered, he said, always in the same whisper, "Goot Yomtof." And that holiday greeting was the total of our conversation for months. He was always gracious in holding the room for me when I began traveling, as you soon shall hear. However, under his own roof he hardly had a friend, although it was evident he needed one. Even now I can hear the sad music he played, slow Romanian-sounding dances, and I can smell the odor of the stew or goulash he often cooked, wafting up from the basement when I entered the lobby; once or twice I descended the stairs to befriend him, and also because I needed a friend. But I never got all the way to his door.

The building was a place of transience and dilapidation, hiding and flight, and I felt instantly at home. Into these rooms I moved my boxes from Big Lou's apartment. If what now occurred seems confused, a step toward Nineveh but also a step toward the beautiful godlessness of Buddhism, it is because the Jonah of our story—the prophet's and my own—was indeed suspended between the two callings. And so my life too took its next turn.

I often rode the 104 bus up and down Broadway from terminus to terminus. I felt soothed by the bus's movement, calmed by travel and transport of any kind. I applied for several jobs at the airport on the night shift. Although no one was hiring, I lingered at La Guardia and Kennedy and roamed the departure gates until I became a familiar enough figure so that I was no longer questioned by the security guards.

Eventually I began to spend my time watching movies, three or four a day. I prowled the Thalia, St. Mark's, the Bleecker Street, and the other revival houses, college film festivals, film societies, and church fundraisers, searching for films in which ordinary people do great and unexpected things. *It's a Wonderful Life, High Noon, Go For Broke, Twelve Angry Men.* Movies in which ordinary people sacrifice themselves for an idea, or for others. Westerns where an isolated hero keeps the bad guys busy so that his amigos can escape to fight another day. I even sat through two hours of a Popeye cartoon festival, the poor sailor brutalized time and time again, his face pummeled, his body twisted and flattened by Bluto until he finds his spinach, eats it, and ultimately triumphs. These hours of lonely viewing often brought tears to my eyes, and the long slow months of self-recrimination and despair began to pass.

I also found sexual relief—with a leggy dental student specializing in gum disease and, later, with a teacher, and two psychiatric nurses, one of whom was Ronnie's ex-girlfriend. When he heard about my situation, he was always calling and fixing me up, a sweet and generous expression of friendship.

Vayehee dvar Adonai el Yonah shaynit. And the word of the Lord came to Jonah a second time.

In the "va" sound of vayehee, in the single letter "vav," which means "and," the Hebrew conjunction carries, as I have indicated, the sweeping sense of time passing. A passage of what could be either hours, months, or years, and always a linkage between past and future. Within the compass of the "vav," empires might rise and fall, geological eras begin to melt away, a child grows up, a prophet stumbles, and governments change. Within such a "vav" Nixon resigned and Ehrlichman and Haldeman were convicted. We had an electrical fire in the rooming house that caused Mickey finally to rewire. In this space between callings, I traveled to Israel and to Asia, and Jimmy Carter became president, and so on and so on.

In 1975 my uncle Abe died, leaving me in his will $3,753. This inexplicable sum makes sense to me only as the money Abe saved in splitting the famous bar/bat mitzvah costs with my father. Thus, these belated bar mitzvah funds ironically subsidized my journey away from Judaism, or so I thought.

I bought an immense backpack, hiking boots, compass, and canteen. I had all the equipment. All I needed was a place to go. It was as if I wanted to travel far away, to regain Tarshish perhaps, but stay in the rooming house at the same time. So, seized by the desire to travel, I did what was now usual for me and began very timidly. I spent many evenings riding the 104 up and down Broadway once again. One night I dreamed I got off the bus and walked into a movie theater showing a documentary about a desert land, and there I was in the film of a place I had never visited.

Shortly afterward I gave Mickey six months' rent in advance and went to the place that had been beckoning not only in that dream but for many years. I had always feared I would not like Israelis, and, alas, I did not. The tensions and unrelieved argumentativeness of their lives beleaguered me. I sought refuge after a month of traveling the country by checking into Pardes Gerim, a retreat-type of yeshiva for foreigners, a clean and tidy place whose main drawback was that every morning you had to study Talmud. After a few days I regained my senses and traveled to Sefad, the great sixteenth-century Kabalistic center. I prayed over the grave of the Ari, Rabbi Isaac Luria. Nothing happened. I only found myself growing suddenly and desperately horny, as if the animal of sex within had fallen asleep and all at once come alive. Perhaps it was the presence of the Shechinah, God's female consort, perfuming the streets and cemeteries of Sefad, that made me feel more lonely than ever.

I prayed at the Western Wall, bought a generous supply of condoms, and booked passage on a Norwegian tanker making stops about the Mediterranean. I stayed two months in Marseilles and a month in the small town of Les Lecques, roaming the beach and staring at the breasts of French women.

In Casablanca I met Yosi, an outreach worker from the Joint Distribution Committee. I actually taught Hebrew briefly at Morocco's only Jewish day school, and then he and I traveled together to Katmandu. I remember we spent Yom Kippur there in a gathering of many other foreigners in a restaurant at the base of a hill on whose crest sat a Buddhist monastery. All during services my eyes traveled up the hill to the monastery, but nothing stirred up there, no smoke from the chimneys and no people moving in and out. I wanted to go up to visit but was told foreigners were not allowed.

Shortly afterwards Yosi and I left and went down to Goa on the Indian coast to get stoned and consult various rinpoches, gurus, and teachers who might enlighten us. My hair was down below my shoulder blades by then and I had absorbed large amounts of marijuana and LSD. But not even the easy availability of drugs was sufficient to make us linger long in India. Hinduism's gods and goddesses seemed even more hopelessly confused than the bureaucrats in the American embassies and the officials at the train stations. Yosi got into some drug trouble because he was more brash than I. When he was released from two days in jail, we were both asked to leave the country. He went off, I am not sure where, and I, with the funds I had left, went to my last stop, Japan.

Here too, because I could not articulate to myself what it was I was looking for, I have few recollections of the places I visited, although I believe I did stop at a Zen monastery to hear the monks chant their gathas—their beautiful Buddhist brachot—as they moved along, begging in their ceremonial line from the monastery down to the town. This moved me deeply. But my money was running out. To travel well, one must be open to discovery and change, one must have cultivated at least a touch of Great Mindfulness. But I was still in flight.

When I returned to the rooming house, Mickey, who opened the door to the room, said, "I cleaned and dusted for you. I know you use drugs like the Cubans, you are an embarrassment to me as a Jew, but I like having you around." I embraced him and inexplicably broke into tears. The room had not changed and it was somehow filled, I can not explain quite how, with the aura of Mickey's love. It was as if only a moment had passed, one inhalation and one exhalation, between my going halfway around the world and back to my room. I was home.

I dropped my backpack, took the handful of change I had left in my tallis bag on the bed, and went down to the phone on the first floor. After calls to the Questions as frantic as those I had made to corral attendees to Junior Cong, I finally reached Ronnie in New Jersey. I had not written my friends more than one or two postcards from Israel or Asia and now I felt desperate to reconnect with them. I found that Ronnie already had two kids with Dahlia and was making a good life for himself as a temple rabbi. I felt pleasure for him but no envy when I visited, particularly on my first High Holidays back in America. Whatever life was with-holding or keeping in the wings for me, I was sure of very little except that the suburban rabbinical path was not going to be mine.

I continued to have intimations, as I have said, that I was somehow reliving the prophet's life in modern form. But I could not say much else. Something had to be coming around the spiritual bend, as it were, and patience was being required. But did I have enough? I did not entertain the idea of wrapping myself in a tunic or kaffiyeh and joining the margin-ally sane walkers jabbering on Broadway. But there was the potential of breakdown, and what kept me from it, I have no doubt, was that I was waiting for a clear word, a sense of dawning or direction or light within; if I could just endure, some sort of articulation had to register. But where? When? How?

This prospect continued to be both terrifying and uplifting. I had a number of semi-gratifying but short-lived relationships with women who had both intellectual and physical gifts. I still occasionally taught Hebrew school, scrambling for a class usually after the bank had written me about my most recent bounced check. Otherwise I groped in a fog of no self-knowledge. I took a few classes in karate and then used the few moves and katas I mastered to catch the attention of my bored Hebrew-school students. I taught them to count in Japanese as I taught them the Hebrew. Likewise with the body parts. I was particularly moved by the chi force, the cry that emerges from your innermost self as you finish a kata or finally make the strike with the knife hand and call it out—chiyaaaaa!— the force that is within you and the universe. Its etymological relationship to *chaim*, the Hebrew word for life, might be crackpot, but now and then it did make for a good lesson.

My contact with the other Questions began to grow less and less frequent. Arthur had left his job in Illinois after some sort of disagreement about salary. He wrote from his new pulpit in a little community in California that he was thriving, but we were estranged by the distance. Big Lou had disappeared into the wilds of educational psychology, I believe, and got a job somewhere in North Carolina, marrying, finally, a non-Jewish woman from a family that manufactured textiles. I spoke to him every six months or so and found out that in spite of his well-paying secular job and non-Jewish wife, Big Lou was still teaching in several of the Hebrew schools of Winston-Salem, Raleigh, and eastern North Carolina—to the consternation of his wife's family. He said it was a habit, just a part of his routine he would find unsettling to give up, like shaving. I knew exactly what he meant.

When I discovered I had only nineteen dollars in my drawer, and the weekly rent in the rooming house being twenty-five, I resolved to answer an advertisement for restaurant help. I had found I enjoyed the occasional physical work I had done over the past year through the temporary agencies— a week at a coffin factory near Wall Street, another week as a cleaner for a company servicing pizza and other industrial ovens. The particular advertisement I answered turned out to be for kitchen help at the B & G Restaurant, a vegetarian and dairy place downtown in what used to be the Jewish neighborhood.

It was a large, airy, and chaotic operation patronized by palsied Jewish men and women and young Latinos sitting on chairs always in pleasant disarray and reading *The Forward* or *El Diario* over rice pudding and tea.

One day when the restaurant was particularly crowded, the boss, Mamma Ceil, came over looking for volunteers to wait on tables. Mamma, whose great arms were always speckled with baking powder, took an interest in me. She also noticed that I was the only one in the kitchen at the time able to speak much English.

Thus began my waiting career at the B & G, the profession that served me well for years and perhaps prepared me to wait upon you, my meditators, congregants, and coffee klatsch devotees! Mamma Ceil grew to like me so much she wanted to introduce me to her granddaughter. I lied that I had a steady girlfriend, but Mamma, an astute judge of people as well as kashe, said, "You do not act like you have a steady girlfriend. You act like a married man with a roving eye, yet you say you live alone. You are a mystery. If you weren't such a mystery man, I'd ask you to be my manager."

I remained a humble waiter for another year and was happy, but eventually I took the manager job. I now sported a long ponytail, always neatly pulled back so as not to wag in the food, a large ring with my birthstone sparkling with its curative powers, and a fringed Tibetan vest, whose colorful tassels some of the orthodox customers sometimes mistook for little tsis tsis.

In spite of my various spiritual vestments and regalia, which I changed often, I was still clearly all craving. Nevertheless, at the restaurant at least I had a superficial camaraderie, and I always had warmth and food. Most of humankind over the course of history has had much less. Feeding the hungry was also, in my estimation, not a bad profession for a rabbi, or rabbi manqué, which is what I had now become.

I could have left the rooming house and gotten a proper apartment with the money I was now earning, but I decided to stay put. The permanent impermanence of the rooming house suited me. I would move on when I was good and ready, when there was indication to do so. In the meantime, I experienced puzzling moments of elation in which the whole world beckoned, possibility was endless, and I seemed to dissolve into my choices and experience them all like currents in an ocean. One old man I met at the restaurant, an impeccably tailored diamond dealer from Johannesburg, befriended me, urging me to make my fortune in South Africa. It was a good place, he said, for a smart Jewish boy. I thanked him, but I was not only waiting and managing, I told him, I was also enjoying learning how to cook, and I was therefore fairly happy in my life. This, of course, was a lie.

When I left the restaurant, at around eight each night, and made my way home, I felt my expression slowly begin to alter from the waiter's ever-ready smile into a heavy-jowled sadness. As I turned onto my block, I felt a deep rottenness in my life, empty and cold, as if there were no carryover from the lively life of the restaurant, as if when I crossed over the threshold and began to climb the elegantly polished mahogany stairs of the rooming house, creaking with age, my life suddenly took on a desperate quality.

Occasionally I still picked up a Jewish book. I even began to write a little poetry, always, it turned out, on Jewish themes: a sonnet on an auto-da-fé, another on hunting Jews, one on the York Massacre in England. Like much else that I touched then, it soon grew too depressing, and I gave it up.

I would often climb up to the roof of the rooming house to be alone. I loved the view, especially in October, when the huge harvest moon hung low over the buildings like a stage prop. I looked up on clear nights and wondered what the other side of the moon might look like, the far side where all radio contact is lost. Although I still knew no Zen and had no meditation technique whatsoever, my state of mind was such that I might then have provided an answer to the Zen koan I would later learn:

What did your face look like
Before you were born?

I yearned for and desperately needed to hear the legitimate voice of personal direction, a voice that was my very own. With each passing day my desire increased and my fear of disappointment did too, in equal measure. It seemed easier to hear God, or at least all the old soundtracks of God, than to hear myself. Perhaps this was an occupational hazard of having trained as a rabbi, of having been instructed to listen so much to others in the congregation— I could no longer hear or know myself. Yet I had to know!

One winter night I lay down, slept a little, and rose shortly before dawn. Inexplicably I took down my Tanach, my Bible, and I ripped its pages out one by one, crumpled them, and threw them across the room. Then I somehow went back to sleep. Yet when the alarm went off—it seemed to ring almost immediately, as if to mock me—I opened my eyes, swung my feet onto the floor, which, in the dawn light, was now a wall-to-wall sea of crumpled Hebrew pages, I began to recite the prayer I used to say as a little boy: Modeh ani lifonecha Melech chai vikayom, shehechazartaw bee nishmatee, b'chem-law rabah b'emunatecha. Blessed art Thou O Lord Our God, King of the Universe, Who, with great mercy, has restored my soul.

Some time later, I believe it was 1982—I was thirty-six years old—a new sensation was born within me. How do I know? Because I finally began spending the bright days of that winter away from bars, movies, and the series of superficial relationships with women that were a blur of sameness because I had failed to give myself, to know myself.

Instead, I lingered in the parks and along the streets leading to and from the playgrounds where young couples—settled-looking people my own age and younger—took their children to unwind after being cooped up in apartments on winter afternoons. For hours I found myself staring with a deep longing at mothers pushing their slumbering children in strollers. On the weekends I also began to scrutinize their husbands, enviable men in their freshly laundered white shirts, corduroy pants, and easygoing sweaters, men who proudly held their newborns, or squatted down to adjust a bottle or booties, all these quotidian gestures performed with an effortless and magnificent sense of unspoken social purpose. My attachment to what I saw was so vivid, at times I might have been looking at a life that already was my own and was only waiting to be rediscovered by me and plucked into reality by my virtuous actions. So intrigued and so rapt was I, walking beside these couples, that in the beginning I was chased away by a husband or two, who thought I was up to no good.

There was simply something wonderful about the women's clear skin, which shined, I sensed, with a particularly healthy glow. Such was my imagination that I was certain this tone was activated in the woman only when she was in a marriage with *the* partner of her life. The skin tone of the young mothers, the aggregate aura of woman, man, and child, was one of such healthy settledness, I imagined these fellow creatures of mine were all suffused in a common hormone of stability that thus far had completely bypassed me, the dermatological chemistry of profound love. For weeks it was as if I saw these women everywhere, and once or twice at work it was all I could do to keep myself from leaving the restaurant to pursue a goddess whom I spotted racing past B & G's steamy front windows. Their presence daunted me, tormented me, and yet also excited me in a way I had not experienced before. I was lit up with a bright desire that my own dereliction should cease.

One fine crisp New York evening, as I was walking home on Broadway, I heard my name called. Although you learn in a busy metropolis not to answer each time you hear your name, you well know by now, my meditators, that not all callings are alike. I turned and saw a tall and very elegant woman approaching me. It was Ada Karp.

We had tea in a noisy student restaurant at 116th Street. With such intensity I listened, studying her like—I was about to say like a page of Talmud. I learned that she had married a medical student, now a cardiac surgeon, named Morton, whom I'd once heard about from Brandy. They had lived in San Francisco for five years, where Ada held jobs as a medical technician and Morton studied and did his residency. All the while he was quietly sleeping with nurses, female medical students, and once, she said, with a male ambulance driver in the garage of the hospital. Even though Ada had given up her job as an ichthyologist to follow this abomination of a man to California for the love he had falsely professed and she could have sued him for the value of the support, she chose to let the divorce proceed without contest. I wanted to throw my arms around her and exclaim how much I too had suffered.

A beautiful sandalwood aroma seemed to emanate from Ada's breath, from the plumes of heat curling up from the tea, the restaurant, the entire world! When she opened her knapsack to show me photographs of the stucco house on Potrero Hill where she and the cardiac guy had lived, next door to the rock band Santana, I noticed sticks of incense and a vial of perfume, and beside them a book bound in red. She lifted out the book to satisfy my evident curiosity, and I read the title: *The Fourfold Noble Truths of Buddhism.* The book back in the bag, the conversation continued.

Ada had grown so much more beautiful in the years since school. Her large almond-shaped eyes were impressive as ever, and I found myself staring into them because the mysterious tranquility radiating out was so welcoming, so warming and unthreatening.

Then I examined her skin. Always fair, with an alabaster fragility, the epidermis was positively translucent—not quite the quality I have described above, but of that potential. I was proud she had called my name.

Ada and I began to date and then we made love. She moved beneath me with quiet, silent passion, curving and diving until, as if holding her breath, a great explosion began to build within and she twisted and turned, finally breaching the surface with a great sexual cry. Her skin was white and so perfect to the touch it was as if she had no hair. And I told her so afterward as she lay on the sheet, skin shimmering and filigreed in the slanting light of the street lamp like scales. I studied her long legs, the plain of her great curving pelvis, her wispy patch of pubic hairs, so few of them that she gave me permission to count them aloud.

"You are no longer a virgin."

"And you have learned to close your eyes."

"Occasionally, yes."

Over the months that Ada and I dated, I often watched as she sat meditating in the morning, before bed, and also before we made love. She never seemed to mind my staring as she settled onto her meditation pillow, as if she were rejoining an old friend; instantly I was jealous of that pillow! And in light of what happened at the United Hebrew Alliance of Kleinkill, about which you shall soon hear, it must be said that Ada had been studying Buddhism for many years before we remet, and she seemed the same, yet somehow also dramatically transformed, inside and out.

Her long neck made me want to reach out and touch it as if it were the column of a temple, a site all the more surprising for my having never planned a visit. My skepticism kept telling me that perhaps under my tutelage this phase of Ada's spiritual development, as I gingerly called it, might pass; yet somehow I also knew that wherever Ada had been these many years, it was no place superficial. I thought of the facials Brandy used to crave and that I once bought for her at Elizabeth Arden on Fifth Avenue. It seemed Ada had been visiting a celestial salon for the serene makeover of her soul.

Nevertheless, over one of the many cups of tea and bowls of rice we had begun to share, and after Ada had been telling me about the zendo, the Zen Buddhist Center on 12th Street, and her Tibetan-born meditation teacher, Nawang Dharlo, my rabbi's voice abruptly, and as if on its own, leaped out of my throat: "You are beautiful, you are fascinating, Ada, and all these new ways of looking at reality are also fascinating, but my God! Do you know what you're doing? Buddhism?" Suddenly, and to my astonishment, I was a Jonah railing and quoting Ada one of the rabbis' guiding principles of Jewish life: Al tifrosh at atzmecha min hatzibur. Don't separate yourself from the community.

"But, Jonah," she replied—her tone was the one she often used then, with the perfect breeze playing in it—"I'm not leaving the Jews. I'm simply embracing the rest of the world. That's the story of your book. That's your name, too. That's you. Truth is greater than any single religion."

It was comforting to think in such all-embracing terms, and the simplicity of Ada's response both shamed me and, oddly, also emboldened and exhilarated me. Above all she was challenging me—much as the Book of Jonah challenged the beleaguered Jews of the first century—with its universalist message. I must try, I decided, to alter the turbulent spiritual course down which Ada was headed. And yet, you ask—and rightly so, my congregants—in extending her the hand of our faith was I not putting myself in jeopardy of being similarly swept away?

In my callowness, at which then I excelled, I somehow knew that a dramatic gesture was now required. The hour had finally arrived for me to dust off the rabbinical diploma and to see if a yarmulke would once again feel natural on my head.

"Synagogues of America, watch out!" I shouted from my lonely window. "Repent! For Jonah Grief is about to choose one of you for his own."

Shortly after this Ada asked me to go with her to a teisho, a lecture that Nawang was giving on the Buddhist doctrine of "no ego, no personality." In my ignorance I felt as if she were asking me to enter a church, to genuflect, or to perform an unnamed alien and sacrilegious gesture, the Buddhist equivalent of crossing myself. I, a rabbi! "If at the root of existence," I pleaded, paraphrasing what she had told me, "there is no ego and no personality, then who the hell is lecturing and who's in the audience?"

Ada squeezed my hand and then kissed me twice, once near each eye. "You know you're more than a pretty face," she whispered. "One of these days you better open these big brown things up!"

Her gestures were without any pressure whatsoever for me to participate; yet they hinted that the love and exhilarating sex that had developed between us would either soon end or move on to a new and even more intriguing level. Open these things up? I thought. In order to try on some Buddhism myself? To understand and change my bad habit of taking cheap shots at another tradition? That seemed fair. But what was it about Judaism that made me, in the

face of Nawang, so insecure? Ada did not have to say
much—a quick glance, a smile that seemed to be full
of compassion for a condition I was hardly even
aware of then—for me to sense that it was again time
either to go back into the hold of Jonah's ship and
sleep, or to go up on deck and bail water with the rest
of the crew. It was up to me.

Then off Ada went to her teisho. I didn't go
with her.

That night I stopped at the newsstand a block
from my corner to buy a candy bar. When I glanced
up, there amid the calligraphic headlines of the eth-
nic newspapers I saw *The Jewish Gazette*, which had
been required reading at the Seminary but which I
hadn't laid eyes on in years. Upstairs in my room, as
the floorboards vibrated to the Cubans' loud
rhumba tapes, I slowly ate my candy, sipped a beer,
and read the rabbinical want ads:

RABBI P/T
*If you are currently employed in a lay position and
want to put your smicha to work, send us your
resumé. Easy to reach by public transportation,
kosher shopping, parsonage.*

Parsonage?

STIMULATING, CREATIVE LEADER
*Beth Tefiloh Cong of Coral Gables, a large vibrant
Modern Orthodox synagogue, seeks dynamic
and stimulating creative rabbi to deepen Jewish
commitment and to assist with pastoral duties and*

formal teaching. Salary and exclnt fringes! (Sense of humor also rqrd)

The next day I dialed the Conservative Judaism rabbinical placement line. When the fellow asked how he might help me—a voice I was sure I recognized from Post-Exilic Literature 102—I abruptly hung up. Who would want *me?* How would I describe my work history? I may as well have spent the last ten years in a kind of rabbinical Foreign Legion. Then I thought of the United Hebrew Alliance of Kleinkill, one of Lou's old Hebrew-teaching discards and recommended highly to me by him, that aficianado of part-time rabbinical positions and quarter-time educational directorships. But Lou had mentioned Kleinkill what seemed a lifetime ago. Would they still need a rabbi? And, more meaningfully, would I be able to do the job? I ransacked my wallet to find Lou's number.

Are you still with me, Manny and Rivka, Barry and Diane, my fine Jewish meditators? For here I was, pulled back taut like the arrow in a fully tensed bow. And since it felt to me that there was no archer—indeed my whole life was all arrows and no bow—I, the arrow, simply let myself be released.

I finally telephoned Nathan Demmick, retired dentist, apple orchard owner, and the heart and soul of the United Hebrew Alliance of Kleinkill's twenty-three-family membership. I was surprised at my enthusiasm when he arranged for an immediate interview for me in Kleinkill, a community some two hours directly north of New York City in the Hudson River Valley.

This was no Temple Emmanuel on Fifth Avenue, as you shall soon hear, but then again was I a brilliant Maimonides applying for the job? UHAK was a synagogue just as Lou had described, all but forgotten by organized Jewish life, a shul founded by apple farmers in the early days of the century, whose threadbare purple banner, "Kleinkill Jewish Apple Growers Association," now hung limply, but not without a certain pride, on the tiny sanctuary's walls. For the past fifty years the congregation had been able to afford only student rabbis and itinerant cantors. Situated in the small town of Kleinkill, whose inhabitants either grew apples or worked for the state government in nearby Albany, the synagogue was housed in a brick building on the main street. Next to it was a small parking lot, and just beyond the lot in a copse of twenty-year-old pine trees stood the modest rabbi's residence, built by Nathan's own powerful tooth-pulling hands—a kind of rabbinical log cabin. When I first saw it, I thought to myself, this is where Abe Lincoln, had he been born to Jewish pioneers, might have lain on his elbows by the fire to study Chumash. Because no rabbi had actually lived in the cabin in the fifteen years since it was built, Nathan had been renting it out.

Bordered on the west by a Sweeny's Fish and Chips and, across the street, by two warring convenience stores, the synagogue building, with its modest stoop, looked more like the residence of a family struggling to stay in the middle class than a community's house of worship. You had to look hard to notice the stained-glass Star of David above the entry door and semiobscured by the air conditioner above. The star had been made twenty years before by Nathan's deceased wife. Sixteen-wheelers bound for Albany now roared past on the all-too-close road, and their vibrations had rattled the star into pieces and sometimes made the eternal light inside sway eerily over the plywood ark. Services were being held only once a month and Nathan said he would be happy if I could improve a little on that and attract some new members.

It seemed not a daunting task and our interview went well. Nathan—a rotund man in his early seventies but with the quiet manner of the physically powerful—seemed, to my great relief, quite uninterested in my previous work history. That I was simply there and applying seemed to surprise and please him as much as it did me. He was not curious about details and did not even ask if I had a wife and family.

The job seemed so right for me I got scared. And then, when, after the second interview, Nathan offered me the position—to commence in a month, so that he had time at least to spruce up the log cabin—I found myself speechless. Shaking Nathan's hand, I felt I had just crossed my rabbinical Rubicon. On the train home I felt tears welling up in my eyes. I hurried back to New York City to propose marriage to Ada Karp.

And did she accept, O congregants future and congregants past? And did my incipient Buddhist accept marriage to her incipient rabbi of the United Hebrew Alliance of Kleinkill? And was that marriage and the sojourn that followed, that tenure of love and service at Kleinkill, was this not all as foreordained by the Lord and the forces of karma as it was beautiful? Is it not written in our text of this afternoon:

> *The Lord God provided a gourd that grew up over Jonah to provide shade for his head and to save him from discomfort. Jonah was tremendously happy about the plant.*

It happened like this: Several days later I stood waiting for Ada in what had become my usual spot, beneath the street lamp in front of the zendo. I saw her at the top of the steps turn and bow in the direction of Nawang, the diminutive Tibetan, over whom Ada towered. As she walked toward me, Nawang stepped to the side and bowed my way. I returned the gesture and then he startled me with an additional little encouraging wave of his hand, a kind of American-Buddhist thumbs-up.

O my congregants, how quick I was!

As we began to walk, I asked Ada if she had ever mentioned to Nawang that we were, well, involved. When she said yes, I added, "Have you also told him I would like to marry you?" She kept moving beside me, no alteration of gait, and no word of response. "I love you, Ada," I said, skipping along near her—to all the world I might have been a too-persistent panhandler desperate for her to place something in my cup. "I love you very much, I think I always have, from the first time I saw you the night I looked up from Brandy's closed eyes in the make-out lounge at Barnard, before I knew you were her roommate. There you were up on the landing beside the ficus tree."

"It was a palm tree," Ada said, "a small, bottle-washer palm."

"Whatever it was, you were picking at a leaf, you were up there all alone surveying everyone below. You were wearing something long and white and you had white sandals on; you were up there like a lighthouse above this sea of randy seniors. You seemed lonely to me but also strangely sure of yourself, somehow serene, a slight variation on the way you are now. And there I was hugging Brandy but still feeling very lonely and just not sure of anything. I admired you intensely. I knew you knew something I needed to know. I wanted to walk up there that night to be with you, but of course I didn't. You were daunting, you were fascination at first sight. And I also remember this: To myself I said, I could spend a long time with that person. A very long time trying to figure her out. Emotionally I judge *that* a proposal of marriage way back then. Of course I proposed it to myself, inside my head, and it's taken all these years for the words to come out. Ada?"

She looked at me and I could not tell from her incredulous eyes if she was about to break out into a laugh or move closer to me like the scientist she was in order to have a better look at this unusual, fervent, and loquacious specimen.

After walking another block, which seemed to me to take nearly as long as the recitation of the Eighteen Benedictions, she finally said, "Jonah, what took you so long?"

And I answered, "Is that an 'I will' or an 'I won't'?"

"It's an 'I think we need to talk,'" she said. She took my hand in hers, and we continued across Seventh Avenue, across Sixth. "I think I need to know a little more. For starters, was your proposal sent to you as a message from the Lord to Jonah like last time or—"

"No!" I said. "I authored this all by myself. And"—I took a deep breath here—"I've just accepted a job as the rabbi of the United Hebrew Alliance of Kleinkill. The job comes with a little house. It's outside of the city. In a beautiful farming area that I know you'll love. And there's a Zen Buddhist monastery in Woodstock very near, if you need it."

"I need to know a number of other things," she said calmly, with that voice with the breeze again.

"Shoot," I answered. "Anything at all. For you I'm an open book."

First she wanted to know if I was legally divorced from Brandy. I assured her I was.

"Most of all, tell me if you really know what you're getting yourself into, Jonah. I'm serious about Buddhism. You know that and there's no talking me out of it."

"I would never dream of doing that."

"I'm not so sure you know your own mind."

"Maybe I need you to help me find it." My heart was racing, my optimism propelling me beyond anxieties. "This is an unusual synagogue. Very low key, very laissez-faire."

"Do they know anything about me, about us?"

"I hinted to the president I was planning on marrying. I think it helped me get the job. But no, it never actually came up directly."

"You told him you were planning on marrying before you asked me?"

"I had faith. I was guessing you would say yes."

"But I haven't."

"No, you haven't. But you haven't turned me down, either. I know I'm no great catch, but you're an ichthyologist—"

"Stop with the fish stuff already, Jonah. This is much too serious."

"I've never been more serious in my life." By now we were at Avenue A; we were running out of streets. The river, land's end, was only a few more blocks beyond. We kept walking.

"You felt you had to take a job before you could ask me to marry you? And a rabbi's job?"

"I *am* a rabbi! That's what I do," I said. "Very old-fashioned, very conventional."

"I find this somehow very moving."

I slowed, I stopped walking, I pulled her next to me. It was near a Thai restaurant, I remember, with lots of bikers hanging out in front.

"I love you, Ada," I said. "I have loved you for years. Please accept all my back love along with the future love I offer you. And of course the present. Come with me. Leave the city. There are lots of places to work in the area. There's a big university in Albany. A medical school, laboratories."

"Jonah, why'd you decide to be a pulpit rabbi after all these years?"

It was a good question. And instead of running from it, I told the truth. I said I simply had needed time to work through to my Judaism. That being born Jewish was too easy, that I had slowly been *choosing* commitment. The fact that I'd been fighting it meant I was deeply drawn to the work. Forgive me on this Yom Kippur, but I probably did not tell all the truth because, as always, I hardly knew it all until Ada gradually coaxed it from me. "You want to marry a Buddhist and take a Jewish pulpit at the same time? You've had quite a busy week!"

"You don't want to marry me?"

"I don't want to pull you down."

"How could you?"

"Consider this," she said. "You take a fateful step, you get a job as a rabbi, something you've resisted for so long, and you don't want to face it alone. So you ask me to join you, as your wife and support— me, a Buddhist. A religion expert coming from

Mars to do an objective study might find this confusing. Do you?"

"I am marrying Karp, Ada," I said, declared, practically shouted. "Daughter of Deb and Barney, a one-hundred-percent certified daughter of Israel. Who's going to contest that?"

"I won't hide who I am, Jonah."

"You think I'd ever want you to? You can believe anything you want about Buddha, about the birth and death cycle—"

"Samsara," Ada said softly. "Samsara. You can say it. It won't bite."

"Fine. And you can meditate and I even will meditate with you," I declared, only because it was true, "because I have always liked to sit on the floor and I find this practice humbling and moving."

"You never told me."

"Well, now I have."

"You're just being agreeable. You see? I'll never know now. You will always have me guessing."

"You listen to me, Ada Karp. There's a lot in Buddhism that I like, starting with you. But please never forget that you are a Jew. Technically you qualify, the daughter of Jewish parents."

"You want to marry me on a technicality?"

"You have Jewish feet and Buddhist wings. Those are your words. My guess is that most people at Kleinkill will love your feet. A few will like your wings. Me, I love all of you. Believe me, the kind of shul that will have me will also embrace you. I'm to revitalize the United Hebrew Alliance of Kleinkill.

That's where the Buddhism, the meditation come in. I've thought it through. You can help. You will like the president, Nathan Demmick. You will, you have to! You will."

"Whoa, Jonah," she said. "I haven't accepted."

"This is my life. Share it with me."

"Tell me, would you go to this place and take the pulpit without me?"

"Yes," I said. "I would. But I would be miserable and I'd write you every day. I would send flowers, telegrams, and yammer away at you until I nudged you to join me. I would be a relentless pest."

"You are."

"And I would be desolate," I said, "but I would go without you. Do I have to?"

O, my congregants, she looked very hard at me then. She was trying to find my soul, and marvelously I felt my soul just staying there, not fleeing, but quietly resting in the middle of my chest. That's how I visualized him, my soul, a pleasant, thin fellow in a tuxedo leaning against my heart for Ada to see.

"So why now?" Ada went on. "Why precisely now?"

"Nawang says on his tape that you can look for water in a single well. And if the well seems dry, you can either keep digging or abandon it and go searching for other wells."

"You listened to his tapes?"

"Of course. What interests you, interests me," I answered. "You want me to finish about the wells?"

"Please, Jonah."

"Regardless of whether you stick to your well or go elsewhere, chances are you will find water, he says, or even fail to find it, more or less at the same time. So that's my answer," I said. "It's time for me to fish or cut bait, so to speak. So I choose to fish, Jewishly. To dig, I mean. Forgive the new metaphor."

O, my congregants! Ada forgave the metaphor. She forgave me. And on this Yom Kippur I also ask the Jewish press, those critics who would soon not be very forgiving, who would have a field day of our marriage and our tenure at Kleinkill, for them I ask forgiveness. All together now, the *Jewish Gazette-Advertiser*, the *Hudson Valley Hebrew Messenger*, both now declare your Al Chayts in bold banner headlines for the sin of scandal mongering.

At Avenue B we stopped. I turned toward Ada. My heart was beating rapidly. I was feeling again as if I'd been caught or found out. I didn't want to meet her eye. I thought to myself, I've sounded too good, too pat and facile and she sees through me. I thought: It's all over for sure, you idiot. It's hardly begun and it's already over!

Then she took my face in her hands and moved nearer. Our noses were practically touching. "Are you absolutely certain?"

My answer was an instantaneous "Yes." Ada did not blink. She scrutinized me again. Then she smiled. "Take a long deep breath," she suggested. "Now," she commanded. And I obeyed. She continued to wait. It seemed she could wait forever.

I could not, and I said, "I feel you want me to change my mind, Ada. I feel you are trying to corner me. You want me to *unpropose.*"

"I want you to dig down deep."

"I have dug and I found something. I've found you."

"Don't latch onto me, or onto Buddhism. I don't latch well, Jonah. There could be problems. Big ones."

"Well, of course there could."

"Problems at the synagogue and between us. Admit to the possibility."

"I just did."

"Kicking and screaming you just did," Ada said. "If you're full of doubt and uncertainty, admit it. Wrap yourself in it and fill up with it, Jonah. It's not terrible. It's you."

"Okay, okay," I cried, "I am filled up with it. I'm scared shitless, but I still love you and I want you and I want this job."

"Good!" she said. "I think we're making some progress."

I pulled her toward me then and hugged her until I felt the articulation of her ribs, her small waist, her torso like a pole my arms and legs were wrapped around, and I was sliding. My face was suddenly streaming with tears. I didn't want to let her go. I didn't ever, and then I did.

"Time to meditate now, Jonah, and restore ourselves; when we're clear minded, we can talk again."

"Let's go away for the weekend," I whispered. "I know just the place, near Kleinkill."

"My idea would be the zendo, Jonah. For a full day's meditation. There are cots to sleep on—"

"I was thinking more of sex and a motel."

She dropped her hands from my face to my shoulders, and then let them fall to her side. I reached out to touch her, but the gesture felt awkward and she seemed very far away.

"We'll find some neutral ground and talk, Ada, and then you'll tell me you'll marry me. Maybe."

"We'll see," she said. "I've got to be tough on you first. I've got to know who you are down to the very toes of your being, or it's no deal. And you must know me as well, Jonah. I'm no fish out to rescue you, no ichthyologist to analyze you. You need to unattach yourself from every way you have ever looked at a person, a woman, me. You need to start anew, Jonah. You need to reach down into yourself."

"Where's that? No, I understand. I'm ready to do what you say. I have to. It's right for me. That's why I choose you."

"You were a terrible husband to Brandy. That I know firsthand. And I've had my lousy relationships as well. We don't need to do it again. And in full view of your first congregation."

"Isn't love enough?"

"Don't be so quick. Don't be so facile. Pause and hear a person, Jonah. Take in what's said before you speak your response. That's a nice Buddhist trait. The Jews can use a few more pauses between sentences. Some emptinesses. I'm hitting on you hard. You need to know. I need to know that we're not running anymore."

Listening, I heard my own true tone—both self-parodying and desperate—and I didn't like it. For the first time I began to appreciate the kind of discipline Ada was undergoing with Nawang. The seeing, the patient unrelenting peeling away. If this was not a little satori, a vivid moment of illumination for me, then nothing was. The harder she was on me, the more often I could hear illusion jangling in my head. I heard it and it was like listening to a familiar voice suddenly grown disagreeable and ugly.

My congregants, on this Yom Kippur let us not forget that we can not often escape the illusion of self-knowledge. No amount of confessing will do the trick. No amount of talk, though I suppose we must try. And for that forgive us, forgive us, forgive us. And, Ada, wherever you are, thank you for helping me on my way.

But then she grew silent because, I knew, she sensed I still barely understood her caution. Except in a song, was love *ever* enough? I didn't know then. I really didn't know.

"If we journey together," she said quietly, as we crossed Avenue D, "it won't always be easy, because I won't let you drift off. If I love you, I love you that way. With the truth, Jonah, and without escape from it."

"I know what you mean." I said, lamely. I didn't know, or only a little.

"We'll see, Jonah Grief. We will see what you know."

On the footbridge overlooking Franklin Delano Roosevelt Drive, where we had finally arrived, on a patch of cracked cement obviously favored by defecating dogs and with a view of the East River beyond a worn-out playing field, we stood, our arms around each other, saying nothing. Because nothing more needed to be said. Or so I thought.

A week later, on a late Friday afternoon, we rented a car and drove north to spend the next two days together at an underutilized Catholic monastery about twenty miles north of Kleinkill that rented rooms out to weekend seekers.

I wanted to take Ada to meet Nathan Demmick on the way, but she felt that premature, so we just drove through Kleinkill without stopping. As we did, he happened to be walking along the side of the road near the temple, and I was able to point him out to Ada without his seeing us. He was wearing carpenter's overalls and carrying a paint can, clearly working hard to get the place ready for us. Looking in the rearview mirror, I could see the side of the rabbinical log cabin, with a ladder leaning against it and Nathan about to climb up. He was doing everything himself, with his own hands, and to see it gave me a great sense of anticipation and responsibility; this was not lost on Ada.

Beyond Kleinkill were acres of apple orchards and vineyards, and the road we took brought us around them to a large inlet in the Hudson. Right beyond, on higher ground, the monastery stood, looking like an old crenelated medieval castle without the turrets. We had separate rooms across a spare granite floor. Although I was desperate to make love, Ada wanted the arrangement this way, and the separation without a doubt underscored why we had come to this retreat. The beds were strung with rope, I recall, and the mattress was stuffed with a noisy fiber. Each room had a table, one chair, and a bowl of apples.

The silence was exquisite, and we eased ourselves into it. We walked slowly through the cloister and then down onto a slope of grass that fell toward the river. I can visualize us now, Ada and I ambling down to the great Hudson as the sun was nearly set in the west.

"Have you thought about what I've been saying, Jonah?" she said as we sat knees-to-chest in the grass, and gazed out over the river. "About all the self-hate I hear coming from you?"

I said nothing.

"Sometimes it's a pretty steady stream. I might find that hard to take. What I'd like to know is whether the self-hate is directed at that which is Jewish, or is it anything that is . . . too familiar?"

"Why would I have taken a pulpit," I said to her, "if I were full of self-hate?"

"You tell me."

"There's nothing to tell."

"You told me it's a nonpulpit pulpit. I find that peculiar. What draws you to it, then? That Jewishly it's nothing?"

"It's low-key, yes. What I said was that it's not a suburban bar mitzvah mill, but it's still Jewish, for chrissakes. Excuse that 'chrissakes.' But I've never had such an inquisitor before. And I *am* Jewish. And I intend to be the rabbi. I will not take the job and then act as if I haven't!"

"Please, Jonah."

"What is it you are out to catch in me?"

"I want to know why you find so much wanting in the world and in Jewish life, pulpit or no pulpit. In yourself. Shouldn't the person you've asked to be your partner have such concerns? Isn't it the fact that I'm Buddhist that makes it acceptable for you in some way I don't understand to marry a Jewish or Jewish-born woman? If I suddenly decided Buddhism was just a passing fancy—"

"Stop," I cried. But Ada wouldn't.

"Wouldn't you soon find me wanting, too?"

"If you see through me so much, how can you stand me! Maybe you can't. I don't know, don't know, don't know." My mantra of ignorance. "Look out there," I said, pointing to the big orange bucket of the sun dipping into the hills. "What does the sun know! There's a Buddhist thought for you! Nature is brainless and beautiful and terrible and final." How quickly I had learned to try manipulating Buddhism! How skillfully I tried to get away again.

ALLAN APPEL

But Ada would not go for such ploys. She
allowed me to finish my tantrum, and then she lay
on her back in the grass. "Come, look me in the
eye," she said, slowly drawing me down to her.
"Rabbi of the United Hebrew Alliance of Kleinkill,
look me in the eye and tell me what you see."

"I see you. The eyes, large, brown, beautiful—and
unforgiving . . . shall I continue?"

"Continue."

"I don't want to."

"Question, Jonah: would you jump for joy if I
told you I am throwing in the Buddhist towel and
instead will wear one of those wigs, a shaytl, become
religious, a penitent, a fine new wife for a new rabbi?"

"You've got to be kidding."

"Stranger things have happened. What if I wasn't
kidding?"

"I'd say forget the shaytl part."

"And the rest? Don't you, beneath all your toler-
ance for my meditation and the zendo and the
whole thing, don't you want it all to just go away?
Don't you want to be a normal rabbi in a normal
congregation with a normal Jewish wife?"

"You are normal. I want you just as you are. No
special packages, nothing ordered that isn't
included on the model in front of me."

Ada smiled, definitely a good sign. I thought I
was doing well, but then she came back at me again.

"Okay. There's something else. Look, Jonah.
You see here a woman who has been thinking not
just about Buddhism but within it—are you ready

for this?—celibacy. I don't know why exactly, but Buddhist vows of celibacy are tremendously appealing to me. Celibacy is a great simplifier of life, wouldn't you say? Is *this* the woman you want for a wife?"

"You don't seem much of a celibate when you're with me."

"What do you know, Jonah? What do you truly know?"

"I know what your face and body are saying to me. Beyond that, you're right, maybe very little. I know I can handle whatever problems might arise at this shul as a result of Buddhism." O my congregants, so I thought. So I thought. But celibacy, I had to admit, would be a shaky foundation on which to build a marriage.

"In Brandy you had a wife who wanted sex all the time. In me maybe you'll have one who doesn't want sex at all!"

"Your threats aren't working," I said. "Anyway, Judaism, in its infinite great wisdom, has already incorporated celibacy. As you know, it's the two weeks in each month during the menstrual cycle. So we'll compromise and you can have those two weeks for Buddhist celibacy and I'll call it Jewish religiosity if you want. And then the other two weeks it will be plain hot nondenominational sex. Everybody wins! And by the way," I added, "are you or are you not going to marry me?"

"I'm considering," she said. "I'm considering very hard."

Then we sat there, my congregants, and we meditated in the grass. It was completely quiet except
for the sound of the water. A noisy fly suddenly
landed on my cheek but I did not shoo it or scratch.
I felt my mind more still than it had ever been. A
mouthy person, I felt like talking. I felt like
shouting, "Isn't this wonderful? Isn't this fantastic!"
I felt like ruining it all with words. But I did not.

After about twenty-five minutes, when Ada
slowly came out of the meditation, she reached for
several blades of grass and began to braid them. I
watched with intense curiosity as she finished one
braid, which she turned into an oval shape and
placed carefully, as if she were performing a ritual,
on my knee. And then she braided a second. When
two were finished, she asked, "Are you ready?"

"For you I am always ready."

"In that case," she said, "let the ceremony begin."
In low, grounded tones, she began to sing a deep
Buddhist chant, nothing celestial about the sound
at all. It was a chant about the earth and the sea.
Then she picked up one of the grass rings and,
slipping it on my finger, she recited, in Hebrew this
time: "Hare atah mekudash lee b'tabaat zu k'dat
Moshe v'Yisroel. Behold you are sanctified unto me
with this ring according to the law of Moses and of
Israel. You see, Jonah, I've prepared."

"I do see."

Unable to utter another sound, I took the second
ring and placed it on Ada's finger as she recited the
blessing again—the variant in which the groom

speaks to his bride—and I silently mouthed the words after her. Then we sat there for another half hour, until it was almost completely dark. Neither of us spoke.

Without knowing quite why, I searched around in my pocket and found a book of matches. With this I lit a handful of dry weeds and held them aloft as we recited together: "Blessed art Thou, O Lord our God, King of the Universe, Who has commanded us to light the sabbath candles."

"Anything you want to do, Jonah, is all right. City Hall to make it official, five bucks, a blood test, and a kiss. That's fine with me. Because as far as I'm concerned we are now married. Congratulations to us."

"I don't know what to say," I stammered.

"Good," she said, her lips on mine. "I like you this way—a prophet struck dumb!"

Step forward now, Nathan Demmick, president of United Hebrew Alliance of Kleinkill, and let us cut to the quick. No dillydallying, no more hiding and Jonahing from you on this Day of Atonement. You are a witness this holy day to what happened—do you swear that what you now report, according to me anyway, is the truth and nothing but?

You are president, Torah reader, and the shul's electrician, painter, general handyman, a one-man Jewish band. You are just as Big Lou described you years ago, only older, and who can help that? You offered me $7,500 per annum plus the rabbinical cabin and you threw in free firewood, as was done, I subsequently found out, for clergymen all over the old frontier. And all the wood came from your thirty-two acres of apple orchards that surrounded the synagogue. What orchards you had, Nathan! An acre for each tooth in the human mouth, you said, and as expansive a space to work with as the mouth is small and confining, which is why you retired to Kleinkill. Here you stretched out, you thrived, your trees gorgeously pruned, heavily laden each season with Macs, Golden Delicious, Baldwins, and each tree with barely a tuft of grass coming up at the base. A modest, tiny synagogue, yes, a blip, almost a mistake on the screen of contemporary American Judaism. But also the only synagogue in the country with its very own Garden of Eden.

In that first winter, walking down the long rows of trees with the snow underfoot, Ada and I found such great peace. Our day hikes were wonderful, but those night walks! With the gnarled branches silhouetted against the sky, and the stars above clear as a planetarium's freshly painted ceiling, we felt we had made the best decision of our lives to marry and to be in this place together. Together with you, too, Nathan, and our little Jewish community.

"Rabbi, here, I made you and your lovely wife apple dumplings," Becky Marr used to say. Frieda Gross made apple fritters, and even Adolph Gottlieb, shamed by the women, learned to make something fancy—apple butter—for the rabbi. "What rabbi," I said to Ada, "could have a better contract: a cabin, a wood fire, and endless apple pies?"

When that first year turned into fall, the synagogue steps filled up week after week with barrels of pumpkins and apples that we sold to tourists to raise money to buy a new Torah scroll and to repair the synagogue roof, and Ada found a friend who, for a small fee, rewove the Jewish apple growers' banner. Inside the rabbinical cabin that fall, it was as if Ada and I lived in a bakery on the main street of heaven.

"Time to take another break from that grueling celibacy," she often said to me as we made love like the newlyweds we were. We made love out in the orchards beneath one of Nathan's favorite trees, the big gray one, one of the first planted in the orchard, up at the crest of the hill. Back in the cabin, with cups of steaming cider, we lay naked on the rug in front of the fire.

"Make love with me again?" I said to Ada.

"None of this is as I expected it," she answered.

"How so?"

She thought for a moment and then said, "It all seems so simple."

"Well, we can't afford any letups," I answered. "Otherwise, that old Celibacy will raise her bald head and try to sneak in here."

Bald head? Did I really say that?

My congregants, what is the blessing one says on Yom Kippur on the occasion of cutting out one's tongue?

Ada, it is to you I address this sermon. Had it not seemed to me such a Christian or pagan thing I would have asked you for a lock of your hair. Now I have nothing of you left. No hair, no hand, no finger, no neck, no toenail, no smile, no physical trace but these thoughts. And what is a formless thought? Forgive me, my congregants, but on Yom Kippur, the holiday for the dead, I feel Ada close enough to talk to and I do so publicly in these words.

How can I ever forget my coming in quietly one afternoon in the spring of our second year? You were kneeling on the floor in front of the mirror, wrapped in your saffron hakama. You had your fingers spread out at your temples, and you were shaving what remained of your hair. Before this moment there had been months of occasional nausea and dizziness. I should not have been surprised, but I was. And now there was also a terrible vacant look I had not seen before.

Sensing me there but not turning, you spoke, "I want it all gone. I don't want it going out a clump at a time like a shedding dog. I want a new look. A celibate look, a Buddhist look, a prisoner look. I must be a prisoner of something. Here," you said, "it all comes off and I'll be all of those new things at once."

"I like who you are, just as you are," I said. "Hair or no hair. Cancer or no cancer. No change necessary."

"Touch," you said. And you had me feel your head—do you remember?—with my eyes closed, and you told me, "It's as if my head is a fresh new apple. Bite," you said. I refused. "Bite, please," you repeated. "Put your mouth on my scalp and open wide as you can. I want to hide inside you, Jonah."

I would have done anything to save you. But there it was. Sudden and advancing out of nowhere, the pain and bloating had been no appendicitis. It happened right after the Leders moved in. They were the congregation's first young family in years.

"You have work to do, Jonah," you said to me. "So don't tell Nathan about this, not until you have to. Becky, Rena, there are so many old people here. No need to scare them any sooner than necessary. It will be distracting and shift the focus in the wrong direction."

You were so calm, Ada. Your tranquility was both marvelous and terrible.

"Maybe I'll wear one of those orthodox Jewish wigs after all," you said when the chemotherapy began.

I tried to stick to work. To please you, I tried. We badly needed a sisterhood and without being asked, you became its president. You had three members and I had the Leders' kids and a few of our weekender families' kids in the Hebrew school. I used all Big Lou's mimeographed sheets and taught the holidays and, since I can not sing, you, Ada, came in and taught the blessings.

Your belly began to swell and we made repeated trips to the Albany Medical Center. The synagogue women wanted to know if you were pregnant. And Nathan even offered to come up with a few thousand more for the rabbi's growing family. The baby they thought was inside you was their baby also, they felt. The strains, the wincing that sometimes pierced your smile like a knife, and the cruel illusion. And nobody said you looked radiant, because, of course, it was no baby, but the tumor pursuing its destiny, relentless for your life, my darling, making your liver swell and begin to fail. Soon Nathan, Becky, Adolph, and all the others had to be told the truth.

We continued to take our walks in the woods. We canoed and began to meditate again in the orchard clearings. The meditation was good for the pain. "I'm going to beat it," you kept saying. "I am going to think positively. Every time I look at your face, Jonah," you said to me, "I am going to smile."

Your parents came to help, but what could they do? There wasn't much. Lord, there wasn't much. They asked you if you wanted to go home with them to New York City, to more specialists; you answered, "This is my home."

Remember when that was, Ada? Do you remember, wherever you are now? In November, walking in the orchard with your parents behind us and the sun low on the path in front, breaking up into bright orange patches between the leaves. You were wearing your red parka, and the weather was crisp, the leaves crunching underfoot. I wasn't thinking about your cancer or your dying. Quite the opposite. With death inside you, you were filled with enormous life. It was as if a force were coming from inside you, from where the disease had taken hold in your very center. Walking beside you, holding your hand, I was thinking—I will never forget this, I must never forget this, and must especially remember it on Yom Kippur, this holiest time of the year—I was thinking of the connectedness of all life. Not merely Jewish life, or that tiny community of ours in the middle of the Hudson River Valley, but the life of apples, the aliveness of the grass speckled with frost that lined the paths of the orchard. You ran up to one of the trees and began to kiss the bark and hug the trunk. It was such a heartbreaking time.

Then you regained some strength. The chemotherapy stopped. You began to increase your practice to three and four hours of sitting a day. There were even days when you sat for six, rose up and said, "It's shrinking. I know the meditation is working; the tumor is shrinking."

Was this when Nawang began to come up to Kleinkill? I know you believed that he could help, and you had already begun to hate the false encouragement of the doctors at the medical center, to disbelieve even the science you knew so well. You felt Nawang could focus his meditation, too, so that the cancer, beneath the laser of his concentration, and your own, might disappear.

On the night Rena died, just the two of us were at her bedside in Albany. Do you remember, Ada? By this time the hospital staff knew you well, too! Nawang sat in the car outside and waited for us, the bumbling, nearly aphasic rabbi and his dying wife, to finish our ministering to a dying member of our community. The day we had married each other in the fields outside the monastery seemed like a thousand years ago. It had only been two and a half.

And, yes, that night we also talked to Rena about the Four Noble Truths of Buddhism. Do you hear me, Nathan Demmick? Why? Because Rena asked. And at such a moment, when death approaches, one must answer clearly the questions that are asked; there is no time for obfuscating. Countless rabbis have written and spoken about Buddhism, and so why couldn't we? With this difference: Ada told Rena what she herself *believed:* that all suffering is caused by craving; all craving is caused by attachment; and all attachment is caused by the false notion of and clinging to dualities—I and Thou, you and me, disease and health, life and death—as separates.

Then in my fumbling fashion I told Rena what I could summon from our tradition: we would say Kaddish for her for a year and then after that at Yizkor, the memorial service, and at every Yom Kippur and on her anniversary her name would be intoned at Kleinkill. Her death was an occasion not only to mourn her loss but also to praise God, whose understanding was beyond ours. Rena, a woman without family, would not be forgotten.

Yes, of course this happened right before you arrived at the hospital to visit, Nathan. And no matter what Rena told you, in her dying, or what you thought or feared had happened, Nawang never came to her room, never performed any Buddhist ceremonies with or upon her. She never asked, so why would we even consider something like that? Was this the beginning of your turn against us?

I speak to you now, Nathan. You who acted as if you had discovered some dark secret to find out that the rabbi and his wife were discussing Buddhism with a congregant as she lay dying. There was no performing of secret rites, by the Marrano Buddhist cabal of Kleinkill! A parody of the Jews themselves. No, Nathan, this never happened. A fantasy and fabrication.

But this much *is* true: The rabbi's wife was dying too. And outside, our friend, a Zen Buddhist priest, Nawang, a man gifted in the study of the passage from life to death, sat in the Jeep and himself was reading—do you know what text? Not the *Tibetan Book of the Dead*, as you alleged over and over again, Nathan. Nawang Dharlo was reading Tanach, the Bible, *our* Bible. Nawang's interest was focused that night on our Jewish tradition, just as ours that night was partially on his.

And what, I ask you, Nathan, was wrong with any of this? It was only human. Are you not human, too, Nathan? What was wrong with giving Rena, that sweet old woman, a little of what the other great religions have had to say about death, about life after death, about which I then—and now— know so little? Your own erudition is impressive, Nathan. No simple retired apple knocker you! You know! And because of that, how can you not admit that Judaism, so strong in so many departments, a religion of survivors in life, is exceedingly weak on death? After death, what next? In my view, Jewish theology fails on events that occur when breathing ceases. What do we teach and do, Nathan? A contribution to the shul? A plaque in the lobby and a tree planted in Israel in memory of? No, there must be more than this.

What could I really have said to Rena when she asked me about her soul? About heaven and if there are angels? What are the prospects, she asked me, that I will be reunited with my husband? She was beseeching me, Nathan, and I felt my tongue turn to gauze. "If you don't know, rabbi," she joked—she *joked* when she saw my discomfort—"it's okay." Bless Rena's memory. I found it terrifying to go on, but go on I did. I told her that to the best of my knowledge the angels of heaven were waiting there for her to arrive so that they could taste her apple pie, because even in heaven the celestial bakers could not surpass her recipes. That's what I told her, Nathan. I joked. I apple-pied my way out of my own confusion about life and death according to the Jews.

Perhaps if I had been a better student, if I had been a Brandy, had I not been terrified of Rabbi Greenwald and the other great scholars, I might have learned a little more sophisticated stuff so that I could have provided Rena with some truth and comfort. But would five, ten, even hundreds more pages of Talmud have truly done the trick? I doubt it. If I failed, it is no breach of contract, but because I am a poor rabbi and also because Judaism has its pockets of spiritual poverty as well. You did not think you were getting top of the line, did you, Nathan? On this Yom Kippur, and all others, please forgive me, my congregants, my future congregants, for being so uncharitable this holy day.

So we talked with Rena about letting go. And who better to talk to her than Ada! Why did this bother you so, Nathan? Was it that Ada, then knowing what was soon coming to her, needed Rena as much as Rena needed her? Did you feel, after all the years at the temple, suddenly left out? What came over you? What hardness settled in? Why did you turn on us? Why did you accuse me of conduct unbecoming a rabbi in the dying of Rena Gross? Of subverting our faith? And then of breach of contract? Exactly what did I breach, Nathan? What?

All I had in life was the annual $7,500, the cabin and firewood, the apples, and my beautiful two-and -a-half years with Ada. Why would I want to risk any of that by antagonizing you, I who loved your synagogue? And here's something else: Why all those pleading notes not to let our "scandal" become public? Because it would hurt the community and the Jews, God, the orchard, and everything else under the sun? And this above all: Why, Nathan, did you always spell God *G—d*? Ada always wanted to know. She thought about such small things at the end. No bitterness at all. Only curiosity about detail, about small things, like the motes, the specks, the atoms she felt herself slowly becoming.

"Whatever that dash is doing there," she said one night, "that's where God is for Nathan Demmick, riding on that dash like a cowboy." She thought about you a lot, and yet you did not visit her toward the end, Nathan. On the grounds that it would give the wrong impression, on the basis of some Talmudic text that even I remember: It is wrong for a rabbi even to be *seen* entering, let's say, a pork store, even if the rabbi is there as a plumber to fix a pipe and not as a customer. For an outsider, an impressionable young Jew passing through town, for example, might think, on seeing the rabbi enter, that the spiritual leader was really out for a pork chop! When I pointed out to you that the text referred to a rabbi, not a temple president, you seemed gleeful. "There, there," you cried, "so why doesn't it speak to *you?*"

On these grounds, citing me such a case, with your Talmud open triumphantly before you on the dining-room table of your home, you steadfastly refused to speak with my dying wife, who wanted to make her peace with you. Was the future of Judaism truly dependent on such a heartless gesture, Nathan? Ada certainly forgave you. She said to me—one of the last things before she slipped away—"Jonah, tell Nathan I love his dashes. Don't forget to tell him about his dashes." So there, you've been told. But have *I* forgiven you?

Whatever took over in you, Nathan, to make you say she was a "heathen"? The warmth and enthusiasm with which you embraced us turned as passionately and suddenly hateful, and this Yom Kippur I would like to understand such a reversal so that I can forgive. I know what you said. You said that I concealed, that I obfuscated! That I should have told you about Buddhism, its importance in my wife's life, because a wife of a rabbi, you said, is as important as the rabbi himself, and these things must be known.

However, you never asked, Nathan! You never predicated my hiring on my presenting to you my marital status, my religious pedigree, or the credo of my wife. God forgive me, silence was my friend, yes. But asked, I would have concealed nothing.

For there was nothing to hide! Was Ada's meditation, her deep breathing, a heathenish practice, as you called it? Ada's meditation was to still the mind in order to take in the beauty and perfection of life all around, and later it was also to control her pain that she might be filled with passion for all of life, death included. And when I asked our congregation each sabbath to truly meditate during the Shmoneh Esray, the Eighteen Benedictions of the morning service, it was not some God-denying mumbo jumbo, as you alleged. What you wanted was to hear me ask the congregation to pray for Ada and to ask for God's blessing, but, Nathan, she did not want that. My dying wife's wish was only and exclusively for the congregants, if they so chose, to meditate on the fragility of life.

Was that too a heathenish practice? Frankly, what our services always needed was a shot of meditation, a deeply moving personal focus, not a mouthing, a dull carbon copy, but what the Eighteen Benedictions were originally meant to be, an experience so deep that each worshipper emerges spiritually awake. That's how Judaism got restored in sixteenth-century Sefad and Jerusalem and in Turkey, through meditation and spiritual practice—now barely visible in the Eighteen Benedictions. If that were to happen once again at morning services in synagogues across America, weekly restorations of countless Jews to the ground of their being, then organized American Jewish life could be renewed here for another three hundred years. But because it's not happening in the synagogues, our people are leaving in droves. Nathan, deep inside you must understand this too.

Meaningful spiritual practice, adapted to Judaism, is precisely what Kleinkill needed. That is what I strove for, that is what Ada helped me with. Her dying didn't cause this need, it only made us more keenly aware of it. If I breached a contract or a poorly understood trust between us that was not sufficiently spelled out when you hired me, Nathan, for that I ask you to forgive me. But I innovated at Kleinkill for my congregation and my faith, not primarily for my wife, as you again and again asserted.

And I must add one more item to my bill of particulars, Nathan Demmick: Did you ever consider the effect *you* had on Ada? That your accusations may actually have made her even sicker and hastened her death? Did your turning on us, your severe cold shoulder, could these actually have made the cancer more virulent? Made her desire to resist not as strong when she saw that Kleinkill, as you wanted it, was no longer going to be for people like us? Forgive my pettiness, but the mind and body are one. There, it's out, it's finished!

Now speak up, Nathan. Maybe I have toyed, teased, and ignored you in this text. Perhaps I have set you up. So now it is truly your turn. Speak, defend yourself.

"This Nawang stayed with you every weekend. Every Friday night he came to the shul. So what if attendance doubled! From eleven people to twenty-two is, I agree, nothing to sneeze at. But more people to do what? To hear Lechah Dodi sung to a new melody? To hear your opinion on events in the Middle East? No! They came to gawk at the Buddhists and to meditate. To close their eyes and imagine the Sabbath Bride among us. To focus, to hocus-pocus, rabbi, is why they came! To visualize the female presence of God, you said, the Shechinah, hovering above the bima like a white dove? This is Judaism?

"And why did your priest wear his Buddhist robes in the shul despite my asking him not to? Did you support me in this, rabbi? No, you absolutely did not. Doesn't the man own a plain suit? You should have advised him, warned him, not me. It doesn't take Talmudic genius, rabbi. Just tact and sensitivity and common sense. Were these qualities too much to ask of you? Or should we have forgiven you their absence at this difficult time in your life?

"But here's another explanation that to me rings far truer, rabbi: Was your priest there among us out of more than friendship, more than being a fellow clergyman and friend of your wife? Did he have something hidden up his big wide sleeve? Admit it, you know he did. I don' t care if he loved the Tanach and kiddush and chocolate ruglach. I don't care if he decided to write his own Jewish cookbook. To me that was always a big show, a smoke screen, a deception. The issue is his effect on you. Yes, you, rabbi. Because what was the result: I began to hear three sermons in a row about all that the great Tibetan Buddhist tradition has in common with Jewish tradition. The sefirot of the Kabala and the spheres of Buddhist thought amazingly similar? If I want comparative religion, rabbi, I will enroll at Albany State. I come to shul to pray, to immerse myself in *my* tradition, not to compare and contrast. I come to hear not some long tekiyah-teruah on a Tibetan horn but our own shofar. And then comes the meditation, the cushions, the yoga, and he has Becky and even Adolph and everyone else stretching. No, your wife does the stretching. Stretching is fine, but along with the stretching I know the breathing is sneaked in, the counting of breaths, and the watching of your belly button and inhalations dancing on the tip of your nostrils like a what! At least, rabbi, you might have said, like a dreidel, but no! For me, I would prefer to know what Rabbi Akiba has to say about the parsha of the week. And, if you don't know, rabbi, ignorance is no crime. Is it not as easy to crack a Jewish book as a Buddhist one?"

Is there more, Nathan?

"Of course there is more, and you know it. You can not tell me that any other rabbi in America—I don't care in what synagogue, how big or small, how wealthy or modest—would even tolerate giving his entire congregation a Buddhist puzzle to work on: A monk wants to know what is the nature of the Buddha? So he asks his master. And the master answers, Mu! What is the meaning of this? That, rabbi, is what you posed to the congregation! What do these koans have to do with the Jewish tradition? My God! You were either unhinged or just plain out of line."

More, Nathan?

"You bet! The congregation needed you, rabbi. They needed a young man who reminded them of the children and grandchildren they would like to have. You were a model, an ideal for them. But within a year at our pulpit you started acting like the renegades and Jewish know-nothings that we read about or maybe, God forbid, that we already have in our families. When you started conflating us with the Buddhists, you ceased to be a model,

Grief. You cut your own throat. And you became not part of the solution at Kleinkill, you became the problem itself. And I told you, I told you!

"But were you deterred? No! You kept walking around telling them Mu, Mu. Maybe it would have been better if you had said, Nu, Nu! At least that would be closer to the tradition! Everyone made with the jokes. Mu nu, koan, cohen. But it was not funny. Then came the incense filling up the sanctuary. Who did you ask about the incense and the foreign rituals?"

"There was no ritual committee."

"*I* am the ritual committee. Ask me. And if we have a disagreement, I will go consult another authority. I will talk to a rabbi."

"I am a rabbi," I said to you.

And you answered, "Then act like one!"

And I said, "And what would the rabbi you want me to be do in such a situation?"

"When the entire temple is meditating and knitting zafu covers instead of yarmulkes, doing yoga and huffing and puffing, when everyone is going around cracking their brains about passing through the gates of Mu instead of the gates of Torah, when incense has replaced flowers, and silent meditation is beginning to push out Torah as the centerpiece of our service, then in such a situation you require the rabbi leading such a temple to forbid these activities. If he is instigating them, he should leave. If he refuses, ask the temple president, me, to fire the offending rabbi, you!"

"Which is what you did."

"Yes, eventually. But I was first patient with you, Rabbi Grief. Oh, I was so patient."

"You had to be, you liar. Because I had done precisely what my mandate was. I had revitalized the temple!"

"No, you demoralized us. You created a scandal. You turned us into the Teahouse of the August Moon, you fool! If that is revitalization, who needs it? But there was something more, Grief. I saw what you were going through. I saw your love for your wife, your devotion when she got sick. I too have taken care of a sick and dying wife. Believe me, I know this was not easy. But as she grew more ill, the Buddhism grew. It was everywhere. We are old but we are not dumb, and we saw it all. I talked with the others. You never knew this perhaps. You thought that the women attended the yoga classes and got somehow interested in the Heart Sutra or whatever you were quoting from. But I assure you that was not so. They tolerated you, they only put up with you. The synagogue, what we, the Jewish apple growers and their kin, had been preserving here for decades, was suddenly no longer our synagogue! We looked at each other and we said, 'What have we done?'

"Since I had hired you, I felt worse than the others. I spoke at length with Rena before she died, Rena who, you are right, loved your wife. And with the others. And I told them how angry I was and that I was ready to can you, and to me they said,

'Nathan, be patient. The boy will come round, and look also,' they said, 'at the tsuris in his life, at this tragedy.' So I tried. I bit my tongue, I accepted. I had your Nawang over to my house, with you, for dinner, didn't I? More than once. If my own beloved wife had ever known that fried chicken, made according to her recipe, that I cooked with my own hands would be served to a Buddhist priest, guru of our rabbi and his wife, well, she would turn in the grave.

"I will not quibble that Nawang was an interesting young man. Respectful, and his regard for our liturgy and his interest in creating a Buddhist kiddush was, yes, interesting, and all that. And, rabbi, it was not really that bad either when you had him blow on one of his horns to accompany me on the shofar on Rosh Hashanah and Yom Kippur. It was cute. Who does not like cute? Didn't I go along? Didn't I smile? But down deep, who needed it? This is the point: Instigated and encouraged by anyone but the dying wife of our rabbi, such practices would never have begun around here; or, had they somehow sneaked in, they along with their proponents would be out on their ass! Forgive my French. But for your dear wife we waited."

Thank you, Nathan. You may temporarily step down from the Yom Kippur confessional soapbox I have built for you. Anyone else in the congregation care to ascend at this time?

Well I remember that look in Nathan's eyes and all the small ways affection slowly unravels, a thread at a time, before a dramatic break occurs. I began to feel that termination of my contract was only a matter of time. In short, an ultimatum had been efficiently delivered: Change! Repent, you sinning Rabbi Grief. Or in forty days, in some calculated time, your life will be destroyed. Nathan, by some odd Jonahesque inversion, had become the prophet and I the sinning Buddhist Ninevite.

Perhaps I did not take in all the warnings because I was so focused on Ada. She was suddenly tired and angry, and she tormented herself trying to figure out how she might have gotten sick. Was it from some unexhausted fumes at the research lab she had been working at in Albany? From some chemical she had mishandled during her ichthyological work? A misprescribed drug she took at the suggestion of her ex-husband years ago in San Francisco? Ada found it hard to accept that the cells simply had begun to malfunction on their own.

She was depressed and angry for weeks. Then shortly after she was told she had six months to live, Ada's old self returned just as swiftly as she had lost it. Without the demands of a job, she was now able to increase her meditation to three one-hour sessions per day. Nor did it surprise me that she also began to spend more time at the temple. She zazened and davened and, yes, I did not mind if she placed her pillow on the dais and meditated there in front of the Ark of the Lord. She found that soothing. More than soothing, she found meditation in that particular location, beneath the eternal

light and upon the eternal pillow, the most
powerful meditation experience of all. How could
anyone not allow her? She never did it during
services, Nathan. It did no harm. Should I have
asked your permission, Nathan? Perhaps, yes, I
should. If some visiting dignitary had come and
seen this, though none ever did, maybe a wrong
impression would have been created. If we had had
a full class of Hebrew-school kids and future bar
mitzvah boys and girls regularly in the sanctuary,
then perhaps there was an issue. But we had none.

O, my congregants past, and congregants future
—I hope, I hope! I never saw it as a choice between
the congregation and Ada. Never. She never put it
that way, not once. "I have Jewish roots and
Buddhist wings," is what she always said, believed,
practiced. She lit sabbath candles. She made
Hanukah latkes from organically grown potatoes
and onions. She was there at every Friday night and
holiday service. She helped us walk with the
congregation to the stream behind the shul, there
beyond the first two rows of trees, to throw crumbs
—symbolic of our sins—out on the water at
Tashlich. I remember you with us, Nathan. Ada
walked beside you. You seemed as proud as a father
at his daughter's wedding. You loved Ada. I know
you did. She reviewed books for the seven people
who came to the once-every-few-months donor
lunch. She even took the sisterhood, all four of
them, into the city to see *Les Misérables*. What
duties of the rabbinical wife did she not perform?

I challenge anyone to tell me. And she did all this as she was dying. Who could not love her!

Come, Nathan, let's hear your rebuttal. The tension is great, for these people, my new congregants, are considering me again carefully. They are trying again this Yom Kippur to decide on my worthiness and appropriateness to be their spiritual leader. A yearly exercise every Yom Kippur, the rabbi's great confession, an innovation I have instituted, thanks, in part, to you, Nathan Demmick! I welcome the examination. They need to hear all, do they not, if they are to avoid making a terrible mistake the way you did at Kleinkill? Help them find what I'm concealing, what terrible religious weapon I've hidden on myself only to later unleash on the Hebrew Meditation Circle of Los Angeles. Perhaps I'm a nudist at heart, and I'm only wearing clothes to deceive. As soon as the Hebrew Meditation Circle of Los Angeles hires me, I strip to my skin and then insidiously introduce flagrant nudism into organized Jewish life. L.A.'s first synagogue for Jewish Buddhists in the buff. Come, Nathan. These people have a right to hear your testimony. I coax you up again. Although it is I who evoke you, see how I let you be your full self. Therefore, please, tell them this Yom Kippur afternoon the depth of Jonah's calculation, the true range of his transgressions.

"I will not go so far as to say you are a fraud, but you had the potential. I will say that this flag of Jewish renewal that you wave means only that you are working out your *own* problems of religious identity, and doing so in public. Would I hang my shingle up as a dentist unless I knew from teeth? You should not call yourself a rabbi, a scholar of and a leader in our faith, if you don't believe and you don't know. Sutra shmutra, rabbi. With your readings of the Heart Sutra you broke our hearts. But because Ada was dying you couldn't see our worries, and maybe, out of regard for your suffering, we didn't show them. If so, that was an error. I regret that I did not move more quickly.

"But, Grief, even if we set the personal tragedy of your wife's death aside, did you have any idea of the enormity of what you were doing to us? This was a traditional Jewish synagogue. My father-in-law laid the cornerstone with his own hands in 1920. For what purpose? So that after seventy-odd years you should try to destroy it? Destroy and then justify it through Buddhism and through cancer! What were you doing to us?"

There, that's his voice. I've really given you there the depth of his accusation. And I bow my head this Yom Kippur because Nathan said all that and he meant every word. It was me he was after to admit fault, to repent, to return from my wayward path, to be a Jew, Nathan's kind of Jew. The irony was too much to bear, and I felt as betrayed by my wife's dying and by Nathan's rebuke as Jonah was by God at Nineveh. See in our text chapter 4, verse one:

*And Jonah felt deeply wronged and cheated
and he was burning up with anger.*

Me, exactly.

Then Ada realized her time was nearing; she was
getting ready to die. And she wanted no more of
the Albany Medical Center. We had a hospital bed
moved into the cabin. She planned it all. She had a
sense of when it would occur. "A week," she told
me. "Ten days at the most. Ten more beautiful days,
Jonah, and then mind and body will be separate no
longer. I feel close to being there. No more
suffering. Help me do what I want to do."

I called her parents, and they came and spent a
day with her. By evening, Ada somehow convinced
them to go. Then Becky and Adolph visited.
Fifteen minutes with each temple member and
friend, one visit was all Ada allowed. All came. All,
Nathan Demmick, but you.

I stood by during each of these visits, and I know
what Ada said. She asked Becky to give me a few
more cooking lessons; she was worried I would start
eating junk food after she was gone. She told
Adolph Gottlieb to get more exercise and recommended he take some walks with me in the
orchard. She was thinking of me all the time, as
well as of the others. She did not cry. Her visitors
said that it was an injustice, that they, the old ones,
should die, that it was not Ada's time.

Ada answered, "But it obviously *is* my time."

There were people from Ada's laboratory, and I embraced some cousins whose names I'd heard but never met. They all came through as if Ada was moving down her checklist, which she was. She knew that there is much the dying can give to the living. She saw her dying as a gift and has asked me to see it that way, to tell others as well. I'm trying.

After four days Nawang arrived. Ada was no longer able to get out of the bed to sit on her zafu. So she meditated in the bed while Nawang and I sat on the floor beside her. Three and four hours a day we meditated, in the cabin, with brief breaks in between. Afterward Nawang sat beside Ada and answered questions she had about the passage from life to death. I resented him, yes, of course, but his presence was reassuring for Ada. He knew stories of the deaths of monks and Zen masters, and he told her these hour after hour.

After the seventh day she grew very weak. I panicked and wanted to call the doctor, but Ada would not let me. She closed her eyes and seemed to be slipping into a coma; this is what I had been told would happen, what I had dreaded in spite of Ada's strength, in spite of her instructions.

I went to her bedside and she said in a whisper to me, "Do I die as a Jew or a Buddhist?"

"Live," I said.

"But dying is what I must accomplish today, Jonah. How do I die, Nawang?"

"A sack of skin holding many parts, you return the parts to the earth, molecules to the air and the soil. It is very simple."

"Yes," she whispered. "Simple."

Here I confess that I felt suddenly like driving Nawang from the room, but how could I? She needed him as much as me then. She needed him more.

"You see, Jonah? What was the face of Abraham, Isaac, and Jacob before they were born?"

"I don't know."

"Of Sarah and Rachel?"

"I'm afraid I don't know much, my darling."

"What was the face of Buddha before he was born?" she whispered.

Then her voice trailed off. I kissed her lips, which were very dry. Then they were still.

As Nawang approached, I let go of Ada, watching her fingers slip from my hand to the sheet. She tried to speak again—I believe to dictate a poem, as many Zen Buddhists do, on dying. But they had waited too long. Although Ada's lips moved and although Nawang listened, his ear beside her mouth, pencil poised over a yellow pad, no sound emerged from her.

Nawang began solemnly to recite Gizan's famous death poem:

A thousand hamlets, a million houses
Don't you get the point?
Moon in the water, blossom in
the sky.

He paused, he nodded to me. I don't know if he conveyed wisdom or nothing at all.

"Blossom in the sky," I said. Nawang and I exchanged a glance. We both realized Ada was no longer breathing. I knelt down beside the bed and put my hand on her cheek one last time as he recited, this time from Dogen:

Four and fifty years
I've hung the sky with stars.
Now I leap through—
What shattering

Outside the air was crisp, the sky clear. To myself I recited the Shema: Hear O Israel, the Lord our God, the Lord is One. And then I recited the blessing of no complaint, no contest in the face of death: Baruch Dayan emet, which means Blessed is the true Judge. As moving as these words have always been to Jews throughout generations, Ada did not want them recited over her, so I said them elsewhere, I said them nearby, I said them for me and for Ada. So be it.

I looked inside one last time. Nawang stood beside Ada, as she had asked. Her hands were stretched out palms up, fingers curled. I saw the tight white stockings that keep the feet of the dying warm, visible at the edge of her blanket. This was death, neither Jewish nor Buddhist, just death. Up the slope of the hill toward the apple orchard, the foliage was just beginning to thin in the fall air.

Inside, Nawang, I knew, would now light the pine-scented incense and hold it beside Ada until the stick burned down. Such was the simple purification rite she had asked for. Then Nawang would meditate, joining in what would have been Ada's last meditation on the sack of flesh that is the body: let our concentration begin at the scalp and circulate around the skin, then enter below the epidermis; let the concentration then circle around the heart, around the other organs, until the entire body has been traversed, and slowly think on how the organs work, each one pushing and pulling, filtering, expanding, and contracting; then separate from these vital organs, one at a time, and slowly move out, following the path until the concentration returns again and rests at the same point above the scalp where it entered.

In death, through this meditation and with Nawang's help, Ada was trying, as many of you know, to move from one state of being to another. She was trying to bridge the essential duality of our nature, the self and the other, the separation between life and death which is the cause of our unhappiness. I don't know if she made it, but if anyone could, it had to be my wife. I set this down here, these intimate details of her dying, for the record. Because records are important.

I stood by the door for ten more minutes, breathing in the incense. Then Nawang emerged and bowed toward me. He wanted to know if I was interested in eating some lunch. He was looking for a corned beef sandwich, he said, on rye. I said I was not hungry.

"In that case," he asked, "may I borrow your car? I'll be back in an hour." I gave him the keys. After he got in, he turned and fixed his eyes on me. "Remember to breathe deeply. It is a very sad day, but still a beautiful one."

DALED

AND NOW, MY CONGREGANTS, from chapter 4, verse seven, please let us read together:

When dawn came up the next day, God sent a worm and it attacked the plant so that it withered. God then sent a stifling east wind; the sun beat down on Jonah's head and he felt faint. In his deepest soul he asked for death, saying, Better is my death than my life.

I did think about it in those first days. I wanted to be with Ada, and I thought to myself, how else to join her?

I didn't want to be with people. I couldn't even go into the synagogue. The urn with Ada's ashes sat in the center of the table, and I did not want to leave it, or the cabin. Nathan, Becky, Adolph, Joe Leder, and enough of the other members for a minyan came to the cabin, and we said Yisgadal together. Afterward I tried to pray alone in the cabin as I had rarely done since my boyhood as a star of Junior Cong. But the praying left me empty and cold.

Then I sat zazen early the next morning, the first action on waking, and although I feared the practice would also prove ineffectual, after an hour's sitting, to my surprise and odd sadness, I felt a peace slowly returning. No miracle, but my grief lifted slighty, and it seemed enough.

Eventually I took Ada's urn and walked up into the orchard. There I sat again under our tree. When I finished meditating, I took her ashes and sprinkled them. The wind picked up as I did this and blew some of the ashes back onto my vest, my face, and my lips. I somehow felt Ada in the wind, and I touched a speck or two with my tongue and swallowed them.

There was no traditional Jewish shroud for the body, no service, no funeral, and no burial plot for her in the Jewish corner of Kleinkill's cemetery, where Nathan's wife, Rena's husband—and now Rena—and many others rested. I believe Nathan Demmick never forgave me that Ada's death was somehow not publicly and officially shared with the Kleinkill community.

But how could I offer up my wife's body to help inspire a synagogue or to prove my commitment to my job when Ada had specified meticulously just how she wanted to die and be cremated? Why Nathan couldn't accept this I find impossible to understand. Perhaps I never will. Yet above all else, this led to what then happened, and, in brief, to why I am here before you today.

In the week that followed the dispersal of Ada's ashes, I felt very far from myself. In spite of zazen I continued to feel dazed, as if I had just been catapulted into a bizarre world, become victim of a great theft, and discovered there were absolutely no authorities to appeal to. It hit me on the eighth day, as I shaved off the beard of mourning that I'd allowed to grow: I looked in the mirror and stared at the deep hollowness in my eyes and understood that my great support, my plant, the giver of shade, my kikayon, as they call her in Jonah, was gone forever. Like my namesake again, like the prophet, I left the cabin, took my Bible, my commentaries on Jonah that I'd begun to read again, and my copy of *Zen in the Art of Archery*, and I climbed into the orchard.

I found the tree where we had made love when we first came to Kleinkill, when it seemed we might be here for fifty years together, and I sat under it. I didn't read, nor did I meditate. I just sat. When I heard someone approaching, I was seized by an impulse to run deeper into the woods, and I gave in to it. I got lost, but I didn't care; I wanted to be lost. When I made my way back to the tree hours later, there was a sandwich and a thermos of cider anonymously left for me. That was the first gift. Many more followed.

My congregants, the desire to become a hermit possessed me then. But, alas, not a spiritually fired one, but the wrong kind of hermit, a grief-stricken man who has lost his way. I didn't want to look into people's eyes any longer, and I stayed up among the trees—even now I don't know how many days. The sun and the wind were on me, but, unlike Jonah, I did not feel oppressed or faint. Beaten and somehow being punished, yes. But my new capacity to endure physical discomfort accompanied a desire to receive more of it. Nothing, it seemed, could get me to come down. I drank only water and ate only apples. I smelled Frieda's kugel and Becky Marr's rice pudding, which I used to love, but I had an appetite neither to eat nor to live, only to endure.

I sat there and closed my eyes tight, waiting for whatever was to happen to happen. Perhaps I was up there five days, maybe a week. Nathan later told me—and I vaguely recall—that he climbed up and shouted into the woods where I was hiding to see if I needed a doctor. I said I did not. Once somebody shouted that they were going to call the police. Nathan's voice returned another day and called up to me, asking if, despite my horrible grief and bereavement, I cared at all that my homelessness and eccentric behavior might be an embarrassment to the Jewish community. I told Nathan to leave me alone and to never come back.

Time passed. And then out of the darkness I heard my name called again.

"Come on down, Jonah, come on down. There's some delicious chicken soup for you on the stove in your cabin. And some potato pancakes the way you like them."

"After you eat, you'll have a bath, we'll play some stud, and you'll be your old self again."

The voices, one male and one female, continued, and I listened with fascination: "She was a lovely girl. But it's not the end of the world our boy should do this strange thing to himself."

Mo and Edith, whom Nathan had summoned, took me down from the orchard and put me to bed. I was sick and feverish with chills for a week, but here were my parents, a lot grayer but still taking care of me. I had seen them last just over two years before, when Ada and I had married, and now here they were. Mo had retired from his work, whatever it had been lately, but he was still the same spinning top as always, only stouter, like a dreidel. And still towering above, though I could see the first hint of a stoop, was Edith, her hair nearly white and her face long-suffering, but not without a kind of beauty earned by her patience with Mo. I stared at her and imagined what Ada might have looked like had she survived cancer and lived together with me for another thirty years.

In those first weeks, Mo and Edith didn't seem to trust me to live alone, and I couldn't blame them. They parked their Winnebago beside the cabin and moved right in with me. At least Edith did. She kicked Mo back into the Winnebago each evening around ten, because his devotion to radio talk shows, she was convinced, would disturb my sleep and interfere with my recovery. My mother was certain, as she put it, that Dr. Diet and Dr. Quiet would be the best medicine for me. And apparently she was right.

My parents got along with Nathan well enough and were grateful he had called them, but also embarrassed, I believe. After all, Mo and Edith had not previously been to Kleinkill. I had written them many times with glowing reports about my first legitimate rabbinical job, but they had not visited. It must have struck Nathan as odd that although the rabbi he had hired had an excellent rapport with all the old people in Kleinkill, he seemed to have a tense relationship with his own progenitors.

As my parents ministered to me, I began to realize that our relationship was somehow transformed. I was filled with love for these loony people, my parents, and not only because they had come and in effect rescued me. I was flesh of their flesh. I was their continuance, and such simple insights filled me with a vast new compassion I had not known.

It was not long before Mo, bored by the absence of any serious gambling action in the Hudson River Valley, actually took up sitting zazen with me in the cabin. I loved listening to the cracking of those old bones as he lowered himself into place beside me. I loved his loud "oy vay!" as he good-naturedly got into the half lotus. I had given him my pillow to use, and I settled onto Ada's.

"So now what?" he asked. "My hemorrhoids are in position."

"Count your breaths, Dad. Up to ten and then back."

"That's it?"

"That's it. Keep still and just count. Clear your mind. That's the whole idea. To still the mind."

After five minutes of effort he said, "It ain't exactly blackjack."

"Give it a chance," I told him, "and you'll see. It will be like getting twenty-one, but with a single card."

"That trick I'd like to take to Vegas."

Of course I knew that Mo was humoring me by sitting, but I also saw he was getting something out of it. Shortly after I began to feel better, however, his meditation was replaced by poker, an organized game he established with Joe Leder, Nathan, and Edith, who had become quite a whiz with cards. Nathan was becoming friends with my parents even as I felt him moving fast and far away from me. No matter. I'm sure Nathan told them, during these games, all about my betrayals. That seemed all right as well.

During this period Ada was never very far from my thoughts—she never is—and I found myself trying to respond to my life's questions by posing them for her to answer for me. Uppermost among them now was what everyone else was asking: Could I resume my rabbinical duties without my wife, and, if so, how would things be different?

I decided that I would simply pick a shabbos and go out and try. That first Friday night, as I stood in front of the congregation of about twenty worshippers, I found myself mumbling and then going completely aphasic. I was terrified and wanted to bolt for the orchard to hide once again. I could hear the thoughts inside my head, but it was as if they were all lined up like a band at the back of my mouth and I couldn't make them march out. With an enormous effort, I mumbled something. Everyone quieted down, and people leaned forward in their seats. Perhaps the intensity of my grief or the hermiting up in the orchard made Adolph and some of the others believe that what I uttered possessed an arresting new authority that night.

For the record, my congregants, I believe what I said was only "shabbat shalom," although someone heard "sunyata, sunyata," the Sanskrit word for the Buddhist concept of Nothingness. Perhaps old ears hear strange things, but this misunderstanding was somehow—how I wish I knew the source—conveyed to Nawang.

Shortly afterward, Nawang began to appear for Friday night services, which I, having recovered enough, resumed leading. First he came alone and then, gradually, with more Buddhists. I was happy to have them there to participate with us. They usually sat in the back row. I understood that just as I felt Ada's spirit part of Kleinkill, the cabin, and the orchard, so did Nawang. And the Buddhists' presence made me feel Ada was somehow continuing with me in yet another way.

The services, my congregants? They were much the same as always: We began with silent meditation. Deep meditation. In the sitting position, chairs for the old folks, and for those who wanted them, a neatly arranged row of zafus was always available in back of the sanctuary. Then we chanted, on Fridays, Lecha Dodi, and as the melodies filled up our little shul, we felt the great female presence, the creative and constantly creating force in the universe that makes life of death and death of life. If I in my sermons began to remove the great, bearded, patriarchal, judgmental Eloheem of Judaism and replace him with what I believe made sense to most of the congregants, then I admit to this. Yet it is no sin.

Did I forbid using in our services Adonai, Eloheem, El Shadai, Adon Olam, and all the other traditional terms and names for God? Forbidding is not my line. However, did I say that these words merely stand for forces within us, that they are only part of our minds and our minds perhaps part of a Greater Jewish Mindfulness that is but a subset of General Mindfulness? Well, yes! For so I believed. So I still believe. If Nathan and some others thought that now with Ada gone, I would somehow "come back" to my Jewish senses, as I heard Adolph say one day to someone in the lobby when he thought me out of earshot, well, they were mistaken.

To me the services were as Jewish as knishes, with, of course, something new at the very center, an emphasis on the spirit, on renewing the ground of our being through Jewish and other meditation sources. I was proud of what I'd done, and things went along smoothly for months. Nawang's Buddhist contingent continued to visit, and, along with them, some unhappily affiliated or unaffiliated Jews from the Hudson Valley also began to trickle in for services—in greater numbers than ever before in Kleinkill's history. And for my last Yom Kippur there, did we not have to set up a tent in the parking lot—and pay the fish-and-chips place to close for the day!—in order to accommodate the overflow crowd?

O, my congregants, I was still probably the only full-time rabbi in America living at the poverty level, but I was extremely proud of that and proud also of what I'd done at Kleinkill: combining, as I saw it, the best in Judaism with Buddhism. I had a congregation of young Jews interested in Buddhism, I had Nawang and the Buddhists themselves very keen on Judaism. Not even a year after Ada's death, United Hebrew Alliance of Kleinkill, contrary to everyone's expectations, was still revitalizing the spirits of forty regularly attending members and double to triple that on holidays. We had arrived!

And now came the turning point.

But first I must tell you how much contentment I felt. Mo and Edith, with my blessing, decided to retire in Kleinkill. Flo Krauss, whose restored hundred-year-old farmhouse was across the road, objected to having to look at my parents' Winnebago permanently parked near the shul, but an accommodation was worked out: My parents agreed to sell the Winnebago and find a place of their own in town. Flo, who was a part-time real estate broker, was eager to help. It was decided in the meantime that my parents would park their vehicle down the road several days a week, and always on the sabbath, although they were constantly worried the RV would be hit by a mammoth truck before they could sell it.

It seemed for a short while in Kleinkill that we were all blessed, that everything could be worked out. I was filled with an immense sense of optimism. I missed Ada terribly but nevertheless found myself smiling more than ever before. I embraced Mo and Edith not only because they had given me life, but also because I felt they were going to be my companions in life over the decades ahead, I taking care of them, they taking care of me, as necessary. I felt little interest in finding another wife or in trying to have a child. The temple members too were my extended family, and I was assuming that the continuing exploration of Jewish and Buddhist texts, and appropriately incorporating these in temple services, could keep me occupied for at least several centuries—to say nothing of the sweet smell of the orchard, where I resumed regular hikes along the trails Ada and I had taken many times. All of this gave me happiness far greater than I thought life would ever provide.

Then on a night like many others, when Mo and Edith, having finished playing stud with Nathan, Adolph, Flo, and Becky, were looking through real estate ads and listening to *Religion on the Line* in the cabin, and while I brewed cinnamon-apple tea for us to drink before bedtime, there was a knock on the door.

When I opened it, I saw Nawang, in full priest's robe, standing with two followers, their hands at gasho, bowing deeply toward me. When I returned the bow, Nawang said, "There is something very important to discuss with you, Rabbi Grief. May we enter?"

"My parents are in their bathrobes . . ."

"I know it is late. We could return in the morning."

Sensing their urgency, I was already letting them in. Over tea, this is what Nawang said to me: "We have been observing you for many months, Rabbi Grief. We have been studying you. We believe you are the reincarnation of Labsong Gyotso, one of our greatest tulkas, our teacher and among our wisest spiritual leaders, who died about the same time we lost Ada."

I was astonished. Edith and Mo—my witnesses— turned off *Religion on the Line* and drew near the table to hear what was to follow.

"It sometimes happens that when a person like yourself loses someone so dear, the spirit within him seems to collapse in on itself, which leaves

room for the soul of another to enter. We believe
Labsong is within you, rabbi. Your manner, what
you have been saying during the services we have
observed—all the signs tell us that his voice is
speaking through you. Even the way you breathe
heavily from the midpassage of your nose to the
nostrils, this was Labsong's way."

"My sinus problems tell you this tulka is reincarnated within me?"

Nawang laughed his gentle laugh, but then his
face grew serious. "That is one of many, many
signs," he said. "We have studied this."

"I have a great respect for Buddhism," I answered,
"but this particular aspect of it—reincarnation—is,
in my view, always the weakest. And now I am sure
I am right! This really must be a joke."

"No joke, rabbi."

"Then a big mistake."

"Nevertheless," Nawang said quietly, "it is so.
Everything points to it. Listen: Labsong, in his last
days, used to wander the streets of Dharmsala in
India much like your prophet Jonah that you have
described to me so many times. As on the day we
blew the horns together in the temple. Has this
story not been one of your lifelong concerns, too?"

Mo ran his hand through his white hair and said,
"Will someone please tell us, in plain English, what
is going on here?"

"They think I'm their Buddhist Jonah, Dad.
The spirit of their teacher reincarnated and living
on in me."

"To me you look a little run down," Edith said. "But that's from too much hiking, I think. Not reincarnation. It's ridiculous."

"I'm the same old me," I said to Nawang.

But he now addressed my mother. "Our great teacher's spirit today is living in your son. It is a very subtle thing but true, and powerful. We would like your permission to so declare it."

"Declare it?" I said. "There's nothing to declare."

But Nawang persisted: "This is a matter of great importance for many people in India, Nepal, Bhutan, and Tibet as well. Many in Tibet believe the Chinese killed Labsong Gyotso. To know that he lives on and is within Jonah Grief, roshi of United Hebrew Alliance of Kleinkill, USA, would provide great comfort. Very great."

"Whoa," I said. "If it's my permission you need, Nawang, then you do not have it. I won't give it. I'm the rabbi of a synagogue, by the way, not a roshi."

"The truth does not reside in a single religion," Nawang said. He was quoting Ada to me. I knew it, and he knew I knew it. And I didn't like it. "Labsong was one of the teachers in early dialogue with your Jewish leaders who journeyed to speak with His Holiness, the Dalai Lama, in 1991. Labsong had an affinity for Jewish-style teaching. To all of us who are studying this matter, his choice of body in which to reside seems perfection."

"Perfection to you is still a huge error, as far as I'm concerned. I don't accept this, Nawang. It is not only wrong. It goes against my nature."

But still Nawang persisted: "Ada said to me many times what a rare and unusual person you are, rabbi. New spirits often choose to settle in young children, as you know. But sometimes in people like you, Rabbi Grief. Again, we have carefully studied this matter. In a childlike spirit such as yours, with so much of the spirit already familiar to Labsong, it is so."

His assistants smiled and echoed, "It is definitely so."

"How so?" Edith countered. "If we say it's not so?" I felt my parents gathering behind me in the kitchen of the cabin that night, like my defense team, to fight this shocking anointment, as if to say, he's only Jonah, our little boy.

Yet Nawang continued with unflappable calm: "Labsong Gyotso loved apples as you love apples, rabbi. He too lived for many years shunning attention. What is the wonderful idiom from your Bible? Keeping his fire under a bushel? Just like you! When the Chinese drove us to India, he lived in the forest. Where? He chose a wooden cabin, built with his own hands, a place in the fashion of here, where you live, rabbi. And the doctrine in which he made his greatest insights was sunyata, the doctrine of Nothingness. Was sunyata not the first word you uttered when you resumed your pulpit? That memorable night you chose not to speak, but you gave a sermon of a single word—sunyata! This is something Labsong Gyotso would have done as well. In his last years, his hair thinned too, precisely where yours is beginning to bald. Oh, Rabbi Grief, in large ways and small, there are many more signs all pointing to—"

"He didn't give a one-word sermon on Nothingness," Edith said to Nawang. "He was scared to death and he felt like he was having a nervous breakdown."

"Nervous breakdown?" Nawang asked.

"You know, like he drew hand after hand of cards that he couldn't do anything with," Mo explained as best he could. "Nothing added up."

"Nothing?" Nawang's eyes tried to x-ray mine.

"I did not say 'sunyata.'" I felt my heart racing then. "I said the only thing I could think of saying. I probably said, 'shabat shalom.' It means 'sabbath of peace and restfulness.'"

During this exchange Nawang and his assistants, however much they understood of it, only beamed on my parents more. "Nevertheless," Nawang said, "what was heard was heard. Perhaps this breakdown as you described it was the precise moment Labsong's spirit entered and sat down among your own psychological structures as they lay in ruins. Temporarily, of course."

My parents scrutinized me now, their eyes anxious with a lifetime of compassionate but thorough parental incomprehension. The moment had arrived for me to speak up definitively, and I did. "If these rumors, if your contentions are made known outside of this room, there are very serious implications for me and our synagogue," I said.

I stood up. "This must not go any farther than this cabin. It must stop." Then another thought occurred to me. "Anyway, doesn't the reincarnation have to take place within a Buddhist?"

"But it has," said Nawang.

"I am a rabbi, a rabbi, a rabbi!" I yelled at him. "Rabbis are not reincarnations of tulkas!"

"Tulka shmulka," said Edith.

"That way is the door," added Mo.

And so the meeting ended.

But, o, my congregants, the trouble had only begun. Here I was all my life haunted by the ridiculous notion that I somehow was our tradition's version of Jonah in the twentieth century, not a kind of reincarnation, which does not exist in Judaism, but rather a sullen, prophetic role model I had had the poor judgment to choose, and then needlessly suffered, I believe, for many years. Then, when I finally had overcome this illusion, married Ada, and achieved the pleasant, rural, Jewish, meditative life that I had always wanted in Kleinkill, here come the Tibetans to pronounce me a reincarnation of one of *their* people! Couldn't I please be left alone! Let Grief be Grief!

That night I found myself summoning up Ada's image. I visualized her sitting and smiling at me, and I asked her what in the world I should do in this new dilemma. She was silent and beautiful as always, and I sensed only that she couldn't take the matter with too much deadly seriousness. Taking my cue, I tried to ignore everything Nawang had said, and I hoped against hope that it would just go away.

Which, of course, it did not. As soon as the news of our meeting got out, which was inevitable, the life of the temple changed dramatically and, as it turned out, forever. Nawang and the Buddhists began coming to shul in growing numbers. I guess we could have kept them out, had we hired a guard to stand at the door. But apart from robed Buddhists and native-born Tibetans, how could we have distinguished between Jew and Buddhist? And, my congregants, Judaism has no tradition of such suspicious exclusion that I would ever honor. Besides, how would such security measures have looked?

Bad, is the answer. So of course we did not do this, and the problems at the temple only mounted. First, Nathan was confirmed in all his suspicions. My parents' testimony as to how I had rejected the Tibetans' claims made little impression on him. To Nathan I had become, reincarnation or no reincarnation, a Buddhist in rabbinical robes, a charlatan. And that was unacceptable.

The *Hudson Valley Jewish Messenger* sent a reporter, and her piece was picked up by the Jewish Telegraphic Agency. "Buddhist Invasion at Small Rural Synagogue" appeared in two dozen community papers across the country. Nathan was apoplectic.

My parents saw how obsessed Nathan was becoming with me and the temple and did what they could to stay the inevitable. They somehow lured him away for a few days, so that a month after Nawang's pronouncements my parents and Nathan were driving the Winnebago—still unsold—up to Saratoga to play the horses. I meditated a lot while they were away. I prayed while they gambled. I even reached Big Lou and commiserated with him over the telephone as in days gone by. Because he had given me the initial suggestion to come to Kleinkill, I told him I blamed the crisis on him—ironically, of course. Before he hung up, he said, "In spite of all your tsuris, you sound to me like a very happy man. Mazel tov, Jonah, and give 'em hell."

The Saratoga trip was a bust, for Mo and Edith had badly miscalculated that a friendship with Nathan based on cards could have grown into something more solid and potentially helpful to their son. And the proof was that a week after they all returned from the track, several hundred dollars poorer and no longer speaking to each other, I was asked by Nathan to come to his house. There he informed me to expect a visit from an official of the Rabbinical Assembly of America, summoned by him to investigate my conduct.

I was enraged. "Weren't the newspaper articles enough!" I demanded. "You had to convene the Sanhedrin to handle our little troubles here? What is with you, Nathan? Why are you doing this? Why won't you talk to me?"

"I'm way beyond talking," he said. "Something's no longer kosher here, and I'm looking at it."

"So then why don't you just fire me, for godsake?"

"Yes, 'for godsake.' You've answered it yourself!" he shouted back at me. "What you have done here is, in my opinion—" and then Nathan's rage made him forget and break off—"it's a shanda, a public humiliation. But I'm aware that we're not alone. Other Jewish communities are struggling with how to fight this type of thing."

"What *type* of thing? Say it."

"This apostasy, this apikorsus! This whatever you're trying to pass off as Judaism. And therefore they may be able to head off what we're suffering through if—"

"If what, Nathan? If you publicly shame and berate me in front of my colleagues and my parents!"

"As far as I'm concerned you have no colleagues, or you shouldn't, and you won't when the investigation is through with you. As for your parents, they are decent people and I only regret they have to be so close to this. I will not let my consideration of them deter me this time. I made that mistake once when your wife got sick, but no more. So this is the way it has to be. You yourself have brought it on, you have brought it on since the beginning. I saw it but I didn't see it. Now it is clear: first it was the Moonies, then Jews for Jesus; we have seen all this before up here. Now that it comes dressed in saffron robes and smells of incense, and has rabbis like you calling it a return to Jewish spiritual roots, well, to me, it's what it always has been: inauthentic, a non-Judaism, a heresy, and it needs to be exposed for all to see."

I guess I could have fled at that point, as I'd fled so many times before. Certainly the thought occurred to me to throw in the rabbinical towel. But something also made me very sane then, as Nathan spoke in such a fury and trembling of voice that I was afraid he would have a heart attack in front of me. I thought: What could this "investigation" really expose? What had I done that was not from my heart? What reason to fear it? What did I have to be ashamed of?

Then I felt a patience well up in me to match Nathan's anger. As I watched him attack me, shaking and leaning out of the old dental chair in which he sat, as if at any second he might topple onto the floor (he had six renovated dental chairs in his living room, and this, as it turned out, would be the scene of the "investigation"), Nathan Demmick's whole life came into focus for me: his marriage and hard widowerhood, his pleasure in working with his hands, but, along with that, a strange lack of equivalent strength, dexterity, and suppleness of mind to examine, reexamine, and amend Jewish beliefs and rituals, no matter how established or taken for granted. I told him that except for the Orthodox, most Jews don't believe in the God described in our contemporary liturgy, and that wasn't my personal opinion but the findings of a dozen surveys and a hundred opinion pieces. Suffice it to say that I had marshaled the evidence. So the theological rigidity and the whole essential thinking about God must change, I said (what was there to lose now by *not* saying?), or else Jews are simply being let down by their teachers and leaders. There would be fewer and fewer of us unless we took on this responsibility.

Nathan spinned around in his chair and turned his back on me. Case closed. And still I felt compassion for this man who was, I knew, without the slightest doubt, preparing to destroy me.

When he turned back around, I stood up and without saying another word did what had to be for Nathan a confirmation but for me was meant as an expression of respect and compassion for a fellow struggling human being with whom I was entangled: I put my fingers together in front of me, raised them to my chin, and gave him a deep gasho, a profound Buddhist bow. I will not deny that it was also for me a gesture of liberation.

"You can do your spiritual exercises and bow and bow-wow all you want," he shouted at me, "and I hope you do that for the investigator as well!" As I turned to leave, I heard him say, "Good day, Rabbi Reincarnation!"

At the threshold I paused. When I was sure Nathan was watching I touched my fingers to the mezuzah on his door and I kissed them. Then I stepped out into the cool air and walked back down the road to the synagogue.

The representative of the standards and rituals committee of the Rabbinical Assembly of America arrived a week later. During that time I had prepared my defense and also packed my bags—the trunk that Ada and I had been using as a coffee table in the rabbinical cabin. I packed and cleaned slowly, deliberately, tranquil in my decision that, if I left, this time I would not allow myself to be driven out. Edith and Mo had spent the week in phone calls and visits with temple members, interchanges full of sturm und drang—Mo had even called in and actually reached his beloved *Religion on the Line* in order to try to generate a public relations blitz on my behalf. Throughout I retained a nugget of serenity that got me through those difficult days of waiting.

Yet absolutely nothing could have prepared me to meet my rabbinical inquisitor. My parents had somehow prevailed on Nathan to be permitted to join me at the session, which was held, as I have said, in Nathan's house.

"If you faint, we'll be there to catch you," Edith said.

Although I assured my parents I would not be made to pass out, I almost did when, after I had knocked at the appointed time, Nathan opened his door and ushered me toward the living room. I got as far as the threshold. Only Moses Maimonides, Buddha, or my Ada herself come back to life could have surprised me more.

Three of the dental chairs were occupied—two by my parents and the third by, presumably, the investigator, who looked stunningly familiar. All rose to greet me. And as they did, I smelled a familiar scent. Although more than fifteen years had passed since I had last seen her, Brandy Lee Snyder was still beautiful. She was dressed all in black— long skirt, turtleneck, and vest—and there below her hem I saw the beautifully tooled boots. If this was to be a showdown and now, also, a tense reunion with my ex-wife, it nevertheless, my congregants, began with a smile, an immense one that Brandy beamed on me. The warmth of that smile unglued my feet from the floor, and I walked in.

Her hair was much shorter and she wore granny glasses now, but she radiated the same intense and impatient intelligence. For a moment, beneath the chaotic barrage of memory, I experienced myself as the same old Jonah I had been. I felt a deep embarrassment, as if of shame and failure, but it struck like a sharp pinprick and then was gone, and I soon recovered.

"Look at you!" I nearly shouted. "As impressive as always, and now you're a rabbi?"

"Now that they let us in."

She stood on her booted feet, strode toward me, and we embraced. Mo actually applauded until Edith shushed him up. Nathan, controlling his irritation as best he could, suggested we get down to business.

We all sat, but then there was silence. "I was terribly sad to hear about Ada," Brandy said. I nodded. My gratitude for her remark was inexpressible. Brandy looked directly at me in that way of hers that used to make me feel like the nail about to receive her hammer, but now I saw her gaze only as a reflection of intelligent compassion. "Sometimes it seems that the very best people, the real angels, like Ada, are just too good for the world. She must be at great peace now and out of all pain."

I wanted to absorb these lovely words, to make sure they truly got inside me, so I paused before I answered. I paused a long time. Brandy must have thought I was having a stroke or going suddenly into my aphasic breakdown mode.

Finally I heard my breath leave my nostrils, and I said to Brandy, "I can see you are a magnificent, wonderful rabbi. Congratulations on the person you have become."

"Thank you, Jonah Grief."

"Yes, yes," Nathan said impatiently. "We are all delighted you two are being so civilized and grown up with each other. Although why they send here the ex-wife I'll never know, I'll never know."

"I've explained—" Brandy began to say to Nathan, but he cut her off.

"Look, I accept," he practically snarled. "We are not here to review the past. I trust the Rabbinical Assembly. Let's start."

O, my patient, patient congregants, I will not belabor the to and fro of the long session that followed. A full report has been submitted, as you know, and is always available. Nathan listed his complaints, of which you have already heard an earful: my practices, my conduct, my false, in his view, representation of my beliefs. And throughout Brandy took careful notes. She asked probing questions, she was objective, professional, wonderful. She was clearly not out to wreak vengeance on me for having failed her as a young husband. I felt in that moment I could love her all over again.

"You realize," she said to Nathan as she returned her legal pad to her briefcase, "that I have no power to hire or fire? Rabbi Grief's contract is with you."

"Of course, Rabbi Snyder. But you must be able to do *something* after hearing all this. Defrock him, if he had a frock. A kittel he won't wear, a Jewish prayer robe, no! But this Buddhist shmateh he does. Remember about that?"

"Right here," Brandy tapped her briefcase.

"The tallis is always over the shmateh, Brandy," I said. I felt very calm, but it was not to last.

"Enough, enough," called Edith. "Can't you see Rabbi Snyder's had enough too?"

Brandy checked her watch. "It's not that I've had enough. I have thoroughly enjoyed talking to all of you, but a friend is picking me up soon."

"It's not over," Nathan said. He was growing red in the face. "It's far from over, believe me."

"Whether it's over or not is primarily up to you, Mr. Demmick," Brandy said.

I knew Nathan well enough by now to sense what was coming.

"So this is all the satisfaction I get?"

"What would you have us do? "

"Pass the word about this man. I am not ashamed of saying this: he should not work at another temple. That's it!"

"Blackballing," my father shouted. "Religious blackballing, Demmick. You ought to be ashamed of yourself."

We all walked slowly out of Nathan's house and stood on the lawn, as the arguments continued.

"It sounds as if a decision has already been made," Brandy said to Nathan.

"Maybe it has," he answered, without looking at any of us.

"That, in my view, would be a loss," Brandy answered him. "A great loss. That's my personal opinion, of course, and not that of the committee, to which I'll submit a full report. Because one thing is very clear to me already: There's a lot of healthy innovation going on in Judaism today and a lot right here."

"I've got incense and Buddha coming out of my ears, and this you call innovation?" Nathan was pacing across his grass. "If you do, pardon the disrespect, Rabbi Snyder, but then you're blind too. I am a temple president. Maybe that's not a rabbi, but I am still a leader of the community. The community isn't numerous and it isn't rich, but I know one thing: It is Jewish and I see my job to keep it that way!"

"Jewish renewal takes place in every generation, it always has. There have been a lot of misunderstandings in Kleinkill." Brandy was going out of her way, I saw, to mollify Nathan. "Beneath it all, though, I sense Rabbi Grief truly loves this congregation. My advice is, don't ever forget that, and keep the dialogue going."

"That's still all there is? 'Keep the dialogue going'? Platitudes? People are driving here from miles around to see the reincarnation of this Buddhist teacher inside a rabbi, my rabbi, and you want me to keep the dialogue going? The Buddhists are stealing some of our best minds and maybe in the case of Grief here some of our not-so-best minds, and I should keep the dialogue going? Don't you understand, Rabbi Snyder? A man has a stake in his heart and you rush up to him and you ask him, 'Does it hurt?' Rabbi, the horse is out of the barn. Doesn't anyone understand or care? Isn't anything normal anymore?"

"Mr. Demmick," Brandy said, "change is normal. Religion changes like everything else. Look at me. I went back to school because the Seminary decided women could be rabbis. That's a huge change."

"And maybe, because of it, Rabbi Akiba is turning in his grave."

"I doubt it," I said.

Then Nathan snapped at me. "*You* doubt it? Just who the hell are you! You doubt everything," he said derisively and fervently. "So what is any one single doubt of yours worth, Grief? I ask you that. The answer is, it's worth nothing. Sunyata. Shabbat Shalom. Nothing!"

I didn't like the key into which the argument was shifting. I didn't know what was coming then, but I felt strangely protective of Brandy, as Nathan, having utterly given up on my redemption, turned his sights on her.

"Why do I feel like I am knocking my head against the wall here? Don't you go to a nice normal shul in New York, Rabbi Snyder? And you're married, I presume? Maybe a few kids. That's exactly the kind of environment we want to create in Kleinkill, don't you see?"

"No," Brandy answered him. "No to your inquiries."

"Relax, Nathan," my father now tried. "Nothing's normal anywhere, so now what's abnormal finally comes to the apple orchards. Don't bust a gut, for chrissake."

"So enlighten me," Nathan said, with a sarcastic glance my way. It was as much a demand as a question to Brandy. "Do you have Tibetans at your shul? Has the Dalai Lama been davening with you that you're so calm about this crisis?"

"No," Brandy said, and smiled. And then I saw it coming, the Brandy Snyder gesture. "My synagogue has a few Buddhists, yes, but mostly gay and lesbian couples, one of whom, incidentally, is more Hindu than Buddhist. It's a lovely warm place, and the prayers are almost all in Hebrew. An impressive level of Jewish literacy. You'd enjoy services there, Mr. Demmick." Then she handed him her card. "You ought to come visit if you're in New York."

Then she kissed my parents good-bye and skipped across the street to where a blue Jeep had pulled up and was waiting for her. As Nathan turned to go back into his house, I walked out to the curb and stood there waving good-bye. I felt like a kid, the boy I suppose I truly am inside still, just standing there in awe and waving good-bye to a fascinating performer in my life who has made her one and only stop here before continuing on tour. Then the Jeep surprised me and made a u-turn and pulled up next to me. Brandy lowered the window and introduced me to Karen Levy, who turned out to be a contractor and also the synagogue's administrator.

"I've told Karen a lot about that awful waterbed you built us, Jonah."

"Do you think we'd have stayed married if I had been a better carpenter?" I asked.

Brandy looked at Karen and then back at me. "No way, Rabbi Grief. It was all for the good."

"I really screwed up again, didn't I?"

"Yes and no," Brandy answered. "He's an extremely tough guy. I think you just planted your flag on the wrong ground. It doesn't mean it's the wrong flag, only that the ground's too hard here. It's like the wandering in the desert, Jonah. The old leaders first die out before new ones emerge. It takes time."

"I'm no new leader," I said to Brandy. "You are. You're born to it. Thanks very much. Thanks very much for coming."

"I was planning to excuse myself and send someone else, but then I couldn't resist going to see what's become of my old Jonah. I'll say kaddish for Ada."

"Thank you."

"Keep trying."

"I promise."

"Keep listening for the voice of God."

"It's a full-time job."

"If it comes again, use me for a reference."

I fought Nathan for three more months—not because I thought I could win, but because I did not want to flee again or give the appearance of having been driven out. There were no more investigations—Brandy saw to that—and the week I spent with Big Lou and his wonderful family in North Carolina helped me too.

But the press was merciless, and I was hounded to state precisely what was Buddhist and what was Jewish in my practice and belief, as if a living, changing faith were a container of yogurt, whose ingredients and minimum recommended daily requirements could simply be listed.

Nathan was no longer even civil to me or friendly to my parents. For the first time anyone could remember, he took more than a few days away from the temple; Adolph told us that he'd gone to visit his wife's sister in Florida. He stayed and stayed. For a brief period, temple life seemed back to normal, but of course that was just illusion. And then Joe Leder, a man not much older than I, in his late forties, whose two kids still made up the entire full-time population of my Hebrew school, one day, while moving a heavy pine tree from behind his house to the driveway, suffered a massive heart attack and died.

Suddenly the great and not-so-great Jewish-Buddhist dialogues and debates, such as they had expressed themselves in Kleinkill, came to an end. The press went elsewhere and left us the simple and moving task of comforting Joe's family and burying our dead.

It was while I was sitting shiva, during the mourning period with the Leders, that Ada seemed to come to me again. As I saw her in my mind's eye, she seemed to stare back at me without speaking. That is, I could think of no words to give her to say to me. I was filled up, once again, as everyone was in Kleinkill, with the terrible and awe-filled sense of what a thin thread holds each human life in place.

And that is an important and difficult-to-retain thought, my congregants, that you should dwell on this Yom Kippur afternoon long after I've finished, which will now be very soon. Perhaps it is the most universal and important thought of all.

So, Al Chayt:

For the sin of leaving my first wife in a lunatic flash of prophetic enlightenment, for that forgive me . . .

For the sin of laughing out loud when my friend Martin took his pants down at camp, showing his parts during compulsory morning services . . .

For the sin of translating the Beatles' "I Wanna Hold Your Hand" into Hebrew and then trying actually to sing it at a United Synagogue Youth car wash and variety night . . .

For the sin of not abiding by the traditional distinction that on the High Holidays only sins against God are to be publicly acknowledged, while sins against your fellow man you must deal with every day. But—God help me—what's the difference? For that thought too, forgive me . . .

For the sin of dropping acid with the Four Questions during the foggy haze of the late sixties, and always on the ninth of Av, the day set aside to commemorate the destruction of the temples and the inquisitions and the Holocaust . . .

For the sin of thinking about Brandy's body for years after I should have, for never trying to understand her soul, forgive me . . .

For the sin of using words like, *sin, soul,* and *God* that provide quick pleasure, and comfort, like sugar or aspirin, but that convey only a cloudy meaning . . .

For the sin of never having seen nor even wanting to see *Fiddler on the Roof* . . .

For the sin of superficial piety, easy rabbinical histrionics, absurd rhetorical juxtaposition . . .

For the sin of secluding myself in the sanctuary these twenty-four hours under the guise of self-examination and self-purification . . .

For the sin of all this self-justification and self-flagellation . . .

For the sin of wanting to swing like a monkey from the eternal light and barely resisting a quick leap up, over, away . . .

For the sin of having stripped down in the sanctuary, as my friend did those many long years ago in camp, and sitting naked in each of your seats . . .

For the sin of not loving my co-religionists enough . . .

For the sin of having loved Ada's memory more than my own life . . .

For the sin of contributing to the assimilation and disappearance of my people Israel . . .

For all this, forgive us, forgive us, have mercy upon us.

When the mourning period ended, and, along with it, the opportunity to socialize, my rabbinical life seemed to change. The congregational attendance grew smaller—Jewish and Buddhist. There were still twenty or so people at services, but no one seemed to have the heart any longer either to fight each other or to force compromise. I read from the Torah and conducted the services on the sabbath. It was difficult to get a minyan together any other time. I sat zazen by myself at home two hours each morning. Yet I felt all my practice, my sitting, my praying, and even my work practice, such as cleaning and repolishing all the woodwork in the temple from the seats to the ark, were somehow designed to keep a growing, insistent bitterness at bay.

I thought to myself, I will never ever take another rabbinical job. Each faith, especially when it organizes and incorporates and begins to need real estate, each faith excludes the others. That is in the very definition of faith, no matter the universal pretense. Always exclusion, separation, dualism, clinging, and pain. Never another pulpit, never another wife. I thought of Yosi, of highs and drugs and of the numbing aimless travel of life, and I wondered indeed if Buddhism and Ada had truly been not windows to new vistas but last ledges clutched before falling into the abyss. Ada had always asked me to think on this, and now I was.

As I held on to this thought, I realized I was having a completely new experience: I continued to hold the thought in mind, I examined it, but without getting surrounded or strangled by it. Without self-laceration or recrimination, frustration, or bitterness, I seemed to be accepting and even patient with this condition of elusiveness in which I lived and looked for answers; yet I resolved not to stop searching. And this also was clear: I needed a new beginning, which would only, of course, be continuation. Kleinkill needed the same.

In this state of mind, I received a call from Nawang asking if he might rent the temple once a month for Buddhist services. Such an arrangement is quite common these days, for example, when one group, whose congregational building has just

burned down or is not yet paid for, asks for the loan
of a fellow faith's sanctuary. Our ark and Torah and
eternal light and other religious objects could have
been covered up, and we could have made some
money. Yet I knew that at the United Hebrew
Alliance of Kleinkill such an arrangement would
have fanned again all the furor and tohubohu of the
recent past.

"We are willing to pay generous rent, Rabbi
Grief."

"Do you still consider yours truly Labsong
Gyotso reincarnated?" I asked.

"What is, is," Nawang replied.

So I told him, "Take it up with Nathan
Demmick," and without anger or bitterness I
quietly hung up the telephone.

I took out my zafu and sat. As I began counting
breaths, a remarkable thing happened. I sensed
Ada's presence, not a full-body image of her, but a
miniature presence, like one of those beautiful
Buddhas from Thailand that looks like a dancer,
and I sensed her there right on my nose, bestriding
the tip of the septum. My little colossus, she was in
my every breath.

Words would be doomed to fail, my beloved
congregants, were I to try to evoke for you this Yom
Kippur the wordless and thoughtless sensation of
contentment that filled me up then. A filament of
silence ran from Ada's spirit to me and lit us up
from within. Her dying and my living and my going
on from Kleinkill to my next destination, still

unknown, were separated only by human breath. And yet that was not all. As I have said, words fail me, sermons lie, the letters of the Torah scrolls disappear, the vellum is scraped clean and will hold no ink.

I rose, bowed to my pillow, and then removed my tallis and carefully folded it. As I opened the trunk to return the prayer shawl and pillow, I noticed a piece of paper fallen into the crack. I picked it up, unfolded it, and as soon as I recognized the typeface of one of the Jewish newspapers, I started to crumple it, certain it was an old exposé of the sins of the Rabbi of Kleinkill that Edith probably had clipped and tucked away so I wouldn't have to read it. But I was wrong.

It was your advertisement, my beloved new congregants, which I then read for the first time:

The Hebrew Meditation Circle of Los Angeles, an extraordinary, progressive synagogue located near L.A. International Airport, seeks a highly flexible, eclectic rabbi to enrich and illuminate diverse peripatetic constituency seeking to integrate insights of Eastern religions into Jewish worship and study. Salary commensurate with experience and daring.

In the corner of the advertisement, written in Ada's unmistakable hand, were simple words: "Jonah, why not?"

Why not, indeed! Somehow I knew at once that the job would still be open. It was. And that is how

I have come to you, my congregants old and new, to tell you Jonah's story, the prophet's and my own, on this Yom Kippur.

Kleinkill is now, as many of you know, a Buddhist temple and meditation hall, Nawang its priest. May it thrive and be well. My congregants there, Becky and Flo, Adolph and the Leders, they have all dispersed among the many thriving synagogues from Poughkeepsie to Albany, may they all thrive and be well. And I hear Nathan found the absence of apples in Florida a problem so serious he has relocated to Washington State. I keep hoping he will write to me, and I find I think of him often, always with a backdrop of a beautiful orchard. May they all thrive, both the living and the dead.

And so on this Yom Kippur, as the time for the sound of the shofar nears once again, let us remember that if we take the Hebrew word for "I"—Ani—and reverse the order of the last two letters we spell another Hebrew word—Ain— which means "there is not." It is the negative of the basic verb "to be," the nothingness that lies at the heart of every "I."

Now as the sermon truly ends, let human words disappear even as we use them. We are only the stories we tell. Therefore I ask you, beloved congregants, to turn with me to page 412 in your prayer books and, as we continue the Yom Kippur service, please rise.